THE SMUGGLER OF CAMDEN COVE

ALSO BY KASEY STOCKTON

The God Who Hears

Wm Bingam Hunter

Praying the Bible
Don

→ Patti
→ Monthly Cancer
→

The

SMUGGLER

of

CAMDEN
COVE

(Pray scripture) Psalm 23
"Exposit (the Bible)"
by
Compass Bible Church

Jessica +

LADIES *of* DEVON 5

KASEY STOCKTON

For my office partners:
Alexa, thank you for providing music at my every demand.
And Jon, whose charming distractions made this book take twice as long
to write as it should have.

CHAPTER 1

*A*n early autumn breeze lifted over the edge of the Devonshire coastline and dragged a lock of hair across the back of Pippa's neck. She closed her eyes, breathing in the cool, salty air and letting it cleanse her lungs. The sun beat down on her, but it was no match for the gusts blowing off the sea and driving prickles along her skin. Not that Pippa minded. She hadn't been born near the sea, but it ran through her blood.

Regardless of what her older sister and surrogate mother, Mabel, wanted for her, she would never leave the Devon coast. It was every bit a part of her with its imperfect rocky edges, vibrant yellow ragwort, and pink sea thrift. The swirling water below smashed against the pillar-like rocks standing sentinel along the dangerous coastline, sending a mist through the air that glittered in the sunlight, and Pippa breathed life into her body through the salty air.

She continued down the path which had been forged through time by donkeys carrying their loads of mackerel and pilchards or people heading to the market in Collacott. It wasn't exactly escaping her duties to slip away for an hour or so in the middle of the morning, but guilt swept through her all the same. She had promised to read to Elinor from the old children's primer in the afternoon though, and that should more than make up for her absence during morning lessons.

Her five-year-old niece had a special fondness for *The Little Red Riding Hood*, though Pippa couldn't understand why she loved the story so deeply. It had an awful ending.

Pippa came upon the fork in the path and turned inland, the wind pressing her skirts against the back of her legs as she made her way toward the abandoned cottage nestled in the wood. The further she drew from the ocean, the denser the trees became, hiding the small cottage from view of the narrow path completely, though she knew exactly where it was located. She had been escaping to this abandoned refuge for years.

Pippa had moved to Camden Court nearly ten years ago when her sister had married Liam MacKenzie and brought her to live with them. Her father was a captain in the Royal Navy, and though she'd begged him to take her on his ship when she was younger, he hadn't been able to do so. But Pippa loved Mabel, so the move to Camden Court hadn't been excessively difficult, and it had provided her with new places to explore.

Pippa inhaled the damp, woodsy scent as she trekked further inland. Relentless rain from the previous two days had left its mark in the shiny, lush, still-green leaves, autumn not quite far enough along to alter the foliage. The path was hardened now, the mud crusted and dried.

She clearly recalled the first day she'd taken this fork in the path in search of new trees to climb and had stumbled upon the derelict cottage down the lane. At first frightening in its hollow darkness and with a cracked front door, the quaint, abandoned house had quickly grown in her esteem. It was now one of her favorite places to spend a quiet hour or two in solitude. She loved her niece and nephews, but they produced a great deal of noise.

A dip in the path turned her ankle to the side, and Pippa

dropped on the hard ground, her shoulder scraping the rough trunk of the tree beside her as she fell. A lock of hair slipped free from her knot and fell over her face, and she blew it away, pushing herself onto her knees. She'd been traipsing through this woodland and climbing its trees for more than nine years, and that large rut in the walkway hadn't been there before now.

She glanced up the way and noticed more ruts in the dried mud. The shape and consistency looked as though they were the product of wheels traveling through the wet road, and unease tightened Pippa's abdomen.

Who would be coming to the abandoned cottage, and why would they bring a cart with them?

Pippa brushed her dirty hands down her skirt and carefully picked her way through the trees toward the cottage. A loud pounding noise caught her attention, and she looked up swiftly. A man's voice broke through the stillness, and Pippa jumped from the lane, pressing herself against a wide tree.

"Just there," the man called. "No, over just a bit. The other way!"

Curiosity reared its head, poking at Pippa until she consented to the temptation to peek. She stepped forward, carefully picking her way through the trees until she neared the cottage. In all her years living at Camden Court, the few times she'd inquired about the state of this cottage she'd been met with a severe warning to stay away. The house itself was not cursed, but the man who owned it allegedly carried darkness in his heart.

The man shouting orders swore loudly, and Pippa jumped.

Or perhaps—if the man here today was the absent owner himself—it was less a matter of the house being cursed, and more that *he* cursed. So far, Pippa had heard no less than three disreputable words, and she'd only been eavesdropping for a small handful of minutes.

Movement beyond the foliage continued as the men—for the

first had to be talking to someone—appeared to be putting up a new door. Or they'd repaired the cracked wood and were now returning it to its hinges. Pippa caught the sight of a thin, blond man with his face turned away from her and wanted a better look. But she couldn't very well walk up to the men and introduce herself, not if they were really so bad as she'd been led to believe.

Her reputation wouldn't thank her were she to continue to spy, but Pippa didn't care much for Society's pompous ideas of what held importance. To her, fresh, salty air, the rolling sound of waves, and her family were the only things which held any great importance.

Choosing the perfect tree, Pippa grasped the lower branches and swung herself up, slowly making her way to the midpoint where the branches were sturdy enough to hold her weight and high enough for her to better see Ravenwood Cottage. She wedged herself against the trunk, crossing her ankles where they hung and hoping to blend into the browns and greens around her. Her spencer jacket matched the bark, but her blue gown would certainly be spotted if one of the men cared to look her way.

Unless she climbed even higher to blend with the sky . . . She shook the thought away. That was only likely to draw the mens' attention.

"Just hold it a little longer," the second man called. He remained out of sight, his voice muffled from the door. Pounding followed, and a few short minutes later, the blond man released the door and stepped back.

There appeared to be three men in total thus far: the oldest by a couple of decades, gray from his coat to his hair and seated on a cart, barking orders, a blond, lanky man obeying the orders, and another inside the cottage. Perhaps they intended to move into the cottage and join the community, and perhaps they had a sister Pippa's age she could befriend. The prospect excited her, and she strained to hear sounds of a woman at the pump around the back or inside, singing as she cooked.

The front door swung open and a dark-haired man in his shirtsleeves and a waistcoat stepped through before slamming the door shut, jarring Pippa. He looked to the blond and grinned, and Pippa was robbed of breath, her fingers gripping the bark until her knuckles turned white.

Never in all of Pippa's nearly nineteen years had she beheld a man so handsome. His startling, white grin blazed even from the distance, and his dark eyebrows framed expressive eyes. She wanted to melt into the tree so she could perch from this place and watch the front of the cottage always, regardless of how mad that made her sound.

Could this be madness? Or the beginning of falling in love?

Pippa shook her head. Love? Obviously not. It was nothing more than strong attraction. She needed to manage her feelings before she lost all sense of control and fell to her death. She looked down at the earth, so far away, and swallowed.

Well, maybe not her death, but a broken leg was a broken leg.

And she could not very well find a way to meet this gentleman easily if she had a broken leg.

"Get on with the shed now," the older man shouted, and the handsome, dark-haired gentleman immediately stiffened. He agreed and spoke to the blond man before walking around to the back garden of the cottage.

Could he be a servant? None of the men appeared to be dressed in particularly well-made clothing, but neither were they outfitted in rags. Pippa cared not for what station he claimed, though she knew her sister might have an opinion on the matter. But it wasn't as if Pippa were thinking long-term. She merely wanted an opportunity to meet the man.

Her first objective would be to discern whether or not the handsome man was married, for he appeared to be a good handful of years past twenty, at least. Her second objective: learn his name.

The blond man set to clearing away some of the ivy climbing along the stone exterior of the cottage, revealing where mortar had deteriorated and chipped away, while the older man watched, drinking from a flask he appeared to have pulled from his pocket.

Minutes ticked on as the men worked, and Pippa hadn't caught sight of the dark-haired gentleman in ages. Perhaps if she scooted over on the branch a little, she would be able to see around the side of the cottage or at least find a more comfortable position. She knew the shed to be on the east end of the back garden, and it wasn't too far—

A deep voice came from below. "Do you realize that it is far easier to spy on people with the help of a telescope?"

Pippa yelped, taken by surprise, and lost her seating. She slid off of the branch, only stopping her fall when she twisted and wrapped her arms around it. She jolted to a stop, hanging from the branch with every bit of strength her arms possessed. Thank heavens she had a decent handle on the tree, or she would surely have broken a leg, or worse.

Pippa glanced down and caught the startling light blue gaze of the dark-haired gentleman. She froze, nearly losing her grasp on the branch. Good heavens, this was *not* how she'd imagined their first meeting. Clearing her throat delicately, she set her mind to the task of finding purchase on the branch below with her feet.

It rankled, though, that the man's expression remained surprised while she sought a safe perch. His dark eyebrows lifted, his mouth firmly closed, his hands resting casually against his waist. Should he not at least attempt to save her? Never mind that she would prefer to save herself, she would have *liked* for him to put in the effort so that she might refuse the help.

"If I *had* been attempting to spy," she said, resting her feet on a branch and lowering herself to sit on it. She crossed her ankles again to keep her skirts wrapped tightly around her shaky legs. "Then perhaps I would have already been holding a telescope."

He nodded slowly. "Then may I ask exactly what purpose you *had* in climbing a tree, Miss . . . ?"

Purpose? Drat. She should have fabricated an excuse earlier. Her eye snagged on a bird's nest in the tree ahead of her. "I was trying to catch a nightingale."

He looked up in the higher branches as if searching for the bird. "Ah, of course. How silly of me not to guess that you were hunting for a bird. Were you merely taking a break from your search when I came upon you?"

"Of course. Climbing trees is tiresome work." She hurried to add, "And the nightingale got away from me."

He nodded. "Well, since the bird escaped, and you have no further reason to be in the tree, would you care to come down so I might introduce myself properly?"

Pippa straightened her back primly. "No, I thank you."

His eyebrows lifted higher, though she would have previously assumed that to be impossible. "Let me guess," he mused, a rakish tilt to his head. "You are hoping the nightingale will return?"

"Of course not. Don't be silly. I've merely yet to determine whether or not you are a dangerous man."

The man froze. He crossed his arms over his broad chest, his damp shirtsleeves sticking to his skin in places despite the chill in the air. Sweat glistened on his forehead, and she wondered what he'd been doing to the shed to work up such exhaustion. The last time Pippa had ventured into that area behind the cottage, the shed had seemed to be in perfectly good order.

His blue eyes narrowed slightly, and a thread of interest laced his words when he spoke. "How do you plan to make your decision?"

7

The sly wolf from her niece Elinor's favorite story was brought to mind. The moral of *The Little Red Riding Hood* expounded on the dangers of interacting with strangers—even those who looked rather enticing. She swallowed. This stranger looked *very* enticing.

Pippa needed to be careful.

"Perhaps you could begin by telling me your name," she said, glad she hadn't donned her scarlet cloak today. That would have been far too similar to Elinor's story for comfort.

"William Blakemore."

Her stomach tightened. The man was possessed of a name that was every bit as strong and sturdy as he appeared. William Blakemore. *Blakemore.* Why did that name sound familiar?

"Will you return the honor?" he asked. "Or if you'd prefer not to tell me, I am more than happy to guess."

Well, that sounded far more entertaining. She lifted a hand, palm up, in approval of this scheme. "Please do."

"Sarah?" he asked, his pale blue eyes sparkling.

She shook her head. Sarah? She looked nothing like a Sarah.

"Harriet?"

Pippa scrunched up her nose. Harriet was even worse.

William stepped back a little, tilting his head to the side and running his gaze over her. She felt his blatant analysis to her core. "Is it Emma?"

"Good heavens, no. You couldn't be further from the mark."

"Well, I can continue."

"Please don't. I should think I'll dislike you excessively if you continue to presume names of that sort."

His mouth ticked up in a smile. "Forgive me. I hadn't known they were such offensive guesses."

Motion drew her attention near the cottage, and she looked to find the blond man continuing to remove vines from the walls. Whoever these men were, they certainly appeared to be restoring the cottage for proper use. "Do you intend to stay here?" Pippa asked.

William looked in the direction of the cottage, though she doubted he could see it through the trees from where he stood. "For now, yes."

"Then I suppose we are to be neighbors," she whispered.

"What was that?"

Pippa needed to get home. She could wait in this tree for the man to leave, or she could take a risk. Her backside was growing sore from the branch, and if she did not climb down soon, her feet might fall asleep, and she would lose the ability to make it safely to the ground.

"Will you please turn around, sir, so I might climb down?"

He shifted away at once, and Pippa drew in a deep breath before turning on the branch and methodically climbing down the rest of the tree, peeking every so often to ascertain that his gaze was still averted. When her feet landed squarely on the hard-packed dirt, she straightened to her full height, tipping her head back.

William was tall, much taller than he appeared from above. His shoulders were broad, his waist lean, and when he turned to face her again, his eyes fastened on her like a barnacle to a rock. This had to be the most handsome man she'd ever laid eyes on, and she had seen a good deal of men when Mabel took her to London for a Season earlier in the year.

"It's nice to be on level ground," he murmured, the low timbre of his voice washing over her like an enormous, warm wave.

Oh, dear. Pippa was in trouble.

CHAPTER 2

*W*illiam must have gone too long without speaking to a woman because his conversation with the little slip of a thing standing proudly before him was proving to be far more interesting than anything he'd done in ages.

She watched him shrewdly through the most interesting pair of navy-violet eyes he'd ever seen, looking as though she was prepared to bolt if he made even the slightest wrong move.

He would need to tread carefully, for he wanted her to remain . . . at least until he learned her name. She'd been so offended by his guesses, which brought a smile to his lips. He'd thought they were perfectly acceptable names.

"Well?" he asked, lifting an eyebrow. "Care to tell me who I've spent the last quarter-hour speaking to?"

"My name is Pippa," she said carefully. And then again with more confidence, "Pippa Sheffield."

Pippa. That certainly did fit her better than any of the names he'd conjured. On second thought, William could not imagine a Sarah, Harriet, or an Emma climbing a tree to spy on her neighbors. Because bird-hunting excuses aside, William was positive she had been spying on them.

"Tell me, Pippa," he said, casually stepping closer. "Do all young ladies in this part of Devon climb trees as deftly as you?"

"I would imagine not," she said crisply, her accent brisk and refined. "Though perhaps they could if they practiced."

William smiled. He liked her blunt, honest observation. He imagined her climbing trees all over the county to peek into her neighbors' windows. "Have you had occasion to practice frequently?"

She opened her mouth, but then she seemed to consider her answer, and she took a decided step back. "It was a favorite pastime of mine as a child. I suppose I haven't had the need to grow out of it yet." The edge to her voice dangled a challenge over him like a fishing line—and he a trout—and William was tempted to bite. He wanted to give her reason to step toward him again.

"Are you planning to remain here long, Mr. Blakemore?" she asked before he could speak.

"That is yet to be determined." He said no more, and while he could sense that Pippa wanted to inquire further, he was grateful she didn't pursue the subject. He could not be honest with her about his situation, that was certain. And he had yet to devise a plan with Father, so he needed to be careful about what he revealed.

This peculiar woman was igniting his interest, but William could ill afford to make friends. It would have been wiser to ignore her after he'd noticed her in the tree. In his line of work, he could trust no one, and young women hiding, in trees or anywhere else, were certainly high on his list of people to be wary of.

Despite the impulse to dismiss Pippa as a possible threat, he would need to be watchful. Danger could lurk anywhere.

"Allow me to welcome you to the neighborhood," she said, taking another delicate step back.

Did she realize she was walking the wrong way? He'd much

prefer it if she ceased edging away from him as if he were a predator. Though he couldn't blame her caution.

"I assume I shall be seeing you again?" she asked.

"If you live nearby, then yes. You will likely see much of me."

"Oh, I do live—" She clamped her mouth closed. Her slightly tanned cheeks turned rosy, and William assumed she hadn't meant to freely offer him any more information.

She was either a wise young woman, cautious when facing a strange man, or Ainsworth was already onto them, and she was his lackey. William and his companions had only arrived yesterday—and through the pouring rain, at that. The conditions had been less than ideal for traveling, but they had helped keep prying eyes off the Blakemores on their journey. Surely it was too soon for anyone to have guessed their whereabouts, let alone send a young woman to watch them.

William would need to keep an eye on her all the same. One could never be too careful.

And it was *not* because she seemed like just the sort of young woman he would enjoy keeping an eye on.

"May I escort you home?" he asked.

"No, that won't be necessary. I shan't take up any more of your time." Dipping in a slight curtsy, Pippa turned away from him, and William noticed the dirt smeared over the side of her skirt from her shoe to her hip. Had she gotten in a fight with the tree? His heart had about flown from his chest when he'd startled her and she'd begun to fall, but this dirt didn't appear to come from that mishap. There was no mud on the tree trunk.

Considering the many different ways this interesting woman could have dirtied her gown brought yet another smile unbidden to his lips.

"Shall I see you at church tomorrow?" Pippa asked, turning back and looking at him over her shoulder, narrowing her dark eyes.

Church? Was it safe? He would have to discuss it with

Father later. He hadn't planned on it, of course. He hadn't gone to church since his mother was alive. "I think I'd prefer to leave you wondering."

Pippa halted in the middle of the walkway and turned back to face him fully, her eyebrows drawn together. "Whatever for? You either intend to go, or you do not."

"It's only fair," he pressed, unable to help himself. She certainly did not mince words, so he wouldn't either. He'd enjoyed that faint blush, and the wicked part of him wanted to see just how red he could make her cheeks burn. "How else will I manage to keep you thinking about me long after we part?"

Pippa contained her surprise remarkably well if he had in fact shocked her. She gave him a pert little smile and turned her back to him without so much as a response. She hadn't blushed at all, which was disappointing.

William watched her walk away until she disappeared from sight, and he found himself wondering when he would see her again. He had the oddest notion that when it came to a battle of wits, he'd just met his match.

The hole in the ground at the back of the long shed was nowhere near as deep as it should be, but William was growing weary of digging. Why Father wished for the hiding place to be dug at all was lost on William, for he could not honestly intend to utilize it, not after everything that had occurred in Dorset. Perhaps it was merely a precaution. Even William could admit to the odd discomfort he felt knowing he was without a safe place to store merchandise—regardless of the fact that he had no merchandise in need of storing. He simply felt vulnerable.

It would take some effort, but he had to remind himself that he was out of the game. He was no longer a smuggler; he was a fisherman now. Or perhaps a farmer. He'd yet to decide.

Stabbing the shovel into the ground again, he kept digging, working his muscles to relieve his frustration. If he worked hard enough, he'd be so tired that he wouldn't have time to worry about the predicament Roger and Father had put them in.

It wasn't working. His mind was the ever-revolving wheel of a longcase clock, spinning and turning regardless of how hard he tried to pause it. Every scoop of damp soil he shoveled was a click of time, begging the same question repeatedly. If they were *truly* out of the game, why had his father directed him to dig a hidden storage space in the shed?

William liked to think he was an intelligent man, but even he had shrouded his misgivings with excuses. But standing in the midst of a hideaway for smuggled goods, he could no longer employ denial. It was plain that he hadn't been given the whole of his father's plans.

If he had a choice, William would gladly walk away from smuggling. He would throw himself into the task of becoming the best farmer or fisherman he could, and he would be done with late-night brandy runs and evading the revenue men for good.

His shovel hit a rock, jarring him from his musings as pain radiated up his elbow to his shoulder. He tossed the shovel aside, breathing heavily. He was quite literally standing in the proof that his father did not intend to let him walk away. They may have moved to a whole new county and taken up residence in a long-forgotten cottage on his grandfather's old land, but smuggling was in his blood. He could imagine his father repeating the words he'd said many times before. *All we need is a moonless night and the coast.*

Unfortunately, in Devonshire, they would still have access to both of those things.

Roger stepped into the dim shed and looked around, resting his hands on his hips. His blond hair was darkened by dirt—no doubt a byproduct of wrestling with the ivy on the cottage walls.

His gaze snagged on the small boat hanging from the rafters, one side of the rope broken as it hung perilously lopsided. He flicked his blond head toward it. "That's our skiff?"

Roger was a friend, not a relation. It wasn't *their* boat, it was a Blakemore boat. But that distinction sounded petty, and William tamped it down before he could make his frustration known.

He reached for his shovel again and stabbed it into the dirt at his feet, working around the rock. "Yes. Once the dust is cleared it shouldn't be in too bad of shape."

"Your father truly intends for us to try to be fishermen?" Roger asked, approaching the small rowboat with disbelief. He tapped it, and the rope groaned as the boat swung.

"Yes. Unless you want that coming down on top of you, you best stay clear of it."

Roger took a large step back, grinning.

William leaned his hip against the muddy wall of his hole. "Has the ivy on the house been taken care of?"

"Almost. We can apply more mortar to the walls by tomorrow, most likely. The walls are intact on the south side, so I left a bit of it there." He puffed up his cheeks and blew a breath out, a heaviness to his eyes that revealed how little he thought of their current plan to lay low. "I wonder—"

"Best leave the thinking to me," Father said gruffly, stepping through the open doorway. He dragged his bad leg behind him, leaning heavily on his cane.

"Of course, sir," Roger said, silencing his errant thoughts immediately.

Father looked around the shed and rested his eyes on the boat. "All will come about in due time. If fishing is too unsavory for you, Roger, you can always take up the post of manservant or go back to Dorset."

"Fishing will be grand, sir," Roger said. He was likely thinking that he already had become something of a manservant since coming to Ravenwood Cottage, and William didn't fault him for his irritation. It was difficult shifting from a life of relative ease with servants aplenty to this minuscule hovel without a single helping hand.

But going back to Dorset alone would be dangerous until Roger knew he was in the clear. He would be better off remaining with William and his father for a few months at least until the threat of discovery had worn off and Ainsworth's attention was elsewhere.

Father stepped again, his bad leg dragging on the earth and drawing a long mark in the dirt. "We need a cook. Why don't you go into Collacott tomorrow and hire a kitchen maid, Will? Someone who can prepare dinner and clean a little."

"Tomorrow is Sunday. And anyway, do you not think we should be more cautious? It could be reckless to bring a stranger into our house."

"It hardly warrants the name *house*," Roger mumbled.

Father turned, testing the sturdiness of an old, dusty crate before lowering himself to sit on it. "No. Quite the opposite, I feel. If we are to hide away here, that will only bring further attention to us."

William blinked. "Are we not in hiding, though?" He looked to Roger. The reason they'd come here at all was to protect that man.

"If we were in hiding, William, would I bring us to my father's old house where we could easily be discovered?"

"Again with the term *house*," Roger said as if he could not feel the thick tension in the dim shed. He was more likely ignoring it. "It's more like a cottage. Or a hut, really. Or just neatly stacked stones."

"Do you not fear retribution from Ainsworth?" William pressed.

"Bah! He has no power here. We are in Devon now."

"Which, oddly enough, is still considered England and thus still policed—"

"We can be up and running within a month, easily, and Jack needs a place to drop his next run," Father said. "He'll be coming here."

William's body tensed, his grip tightening on the shovel's wooden handle as the small smile slipped from his lips. William's brother Jack was coming *here*, and he was bringing a ship full of goods for them to distribute. He hadn't seen his brother since that awful, stormy night in Dorset weeks before, and as much as he loved Jack, it had been something of a relief to take a break from smuggling.

William had hoped the break had been clean, that he wouldn't ever have to smuggle again.

Father huffed. "But it won't work if you're spreading distrust among the people of Collacott. We'll want them on our side, son. Not wary of us."

"How am I supposed to manage that?"

Father smirked. "You need to ask?"

Flirt. Father wanted him to spread charm thickly over the patrons of the local village. Don his friendly mask and set to the business of ingratiating his household among the locals. It felt foul and ingenuine, but had he any right to pass judgment on the scheme when it was what he'd done so many times before?

Pippa Sheffield's thin, pleasant face slipped into his thoughts, her expressive eyes full of mistrust even while her tongue slashed sharp barbs back at him. He assumed she'd been waiting for him to prove himself a dangerous man. Hadn't she mentioned that she had yet to determine precisely that? William had the strongest urge to prove her false, to prove himself worthy of her good opinion.

But not unless it was authentic.

"We have a fortnight until Jack plans to make the first drop. We need a good deal of people on our side by then."

"Shall we attend services tomorrow?" William asked, wondering how far he could push his father. He was fairly certain sitting in a church pew was beyond the man's limits.

Father screwed up his face in thought, peering at William through narrowed, dark eyes. "Not a bad idea, Will. Nothing like a good churchgoing man to instill faith and trust, eh?"

"Not what I'd been going for—"

"I like it." Father nodded once, the matter settled. "Tomorrow, we go to church."

The finality of his words rang through the air, chased softly by the groan seeping from Roger's throat. William shoveled the ground again with renewed effort. He slicked the sweat from his brow with the back of his wrist and kept digging until Roger and Father both left the shed. Shadows drew long outside the door, stretching the farther the sun moved in the sky. He emptied his water flask and kept moving, digging until he was near to his shoulders level with the ground. The hole wasn't wide enough, but it was probably deep enough.

Bracing his hands on the edge of the hole, William pushed himself up onto the ground. He sat hard and breathed heavily.

Fine, if Father wanted him to put on a mask of pleasantries and make friends with the good people of Collacott, he could do so. He might feel like a wolf, sneaking into their perfectly cozy congregation and sniffing out the unsuspecting sheep, but he would do his job well enough to protect himself and his family.

For one thing was clear: when they'd been caught and opened fire on the revenue sloop giving them chase on the Dorset coast, Roger's bullet had hit a revenue man, and William had seen Ainsworth's face when it occurred. In a flash, Ainsworth had reached for his fellow officer as the man slipped from his grip and fell forward into the inky black sea, anguish and fear evident in his expression.

Ainsworth's promise to make them pay had not been an

empty threat. He was likely already searching, and he would find them.

Evidently, it was up to William to keep an eye out for trouble.

Because like it or not, trouble was on their tail.

CHAPTER 3

*P*ippa lifted her young niece into the back of the cart before climbing up and sitting beside her. She reached forward. "Hand me the baby, Mabel. It's much easier to climb in with the use of both your arms."

Mabel placed her sweet bundle in Pippa's care before climbing into the back of the wagon and sitting beside her ten-year-old son, James. They kept a carriage that was typically used for such excursions, but with the weather so mild today and the sun so bright, an open-air cart ride to church had been equally appealing to the whole family.

Mabel's eyebrows drew together. "Do you think one of us ought to remain home with Gram?"

"She wouldn't like it," Pippa argued. Their grandmother was too old and crotchety not to have everything exactly the way she liked it to be. She'd grown exceptionally feeble in the last few months and had now reached a point where she had great difficulty leaving her room, let alone traveling out of the house at all. She could not even attend Sunday services, though it clearly pained her to miss them. Though Pippa didn't understand why —Gram could not hear them anyway. She had lost the majority of her hearing long ago and likely hadn't truly heard a sermon in a decade, maybe longer.

Mac finished fiddling with his horse's bridle and swung up into the driver's seat. He leaned back to drop a kiss on Mabel's temple, and she swatted him away.

"Get on with you." Mabel's cheeks pinked in pleasure, and she reached for her baby.

Pippa handed Liam across the way, and he snuggled into his mother's side, remaining fast asleep. At five months old, he took up a large portion of her lap. He was named for his father, but he looked more Sheffield than MacKenzie with his thick, brown hair and small, sloped nose. His eyes were still the hazy blue common in newly born babes, but Mac believed they were beginning to take on the dark navy hue of the Sheffield women. Mabel still argued that they could be any color.

The cart heaved forward, and Mac directed the horse onto the road toward Collacott. The sun warmed Pippa's skin, doing its best to ward off the slight chill in the air. The lane followed the coastline, weaving along the cliffside as the sea stretched out to one side, the rolling, green hills to the other. Pippa inhaled deeply but got a whiff of horse and leather instead of the fresh sea air she'd been hoping for, and she coughed.

"Are you unwell?" Mabel asked.

"No."

"Tommy is unwell, and he couldn't play all week," James said, a small scowl marring his delicate brow. "He has a cold."

"That poor boy. It seems as though he is ill more than he is healthy," Mabel said. "Perhaps we ought to take the Burkes some soup after church. I know Alice set a pot of something to simmer before she left."

Pippa looked up. "We have some bread we can part with as well."

They reached the fork in the road that would take them to the hidden Ravenwood Cottage if they were to veer to the side, and Pippa searched the lane for any sign of William coming from the trees. She was disappointed when the lane remained empty aside from a wagon full of another churchgoing family she knew; there was no sign of William on his way to church.

Mac turned in his seat and pointed in the direction of the cottage as they passed the fork in the road, their cart continuing on toward Collacott. "We have some new neighbors."

Pippa's body stilled. Had Mac met William and the other men?

Liam's tiny wail startled her, and Mabel lifted the babe against her shoulder, bouncing him. "I thought that cottage was uninhabitable."

"I'm certain it needs a lot of work," Mac said.

Mabel's eyebrows knit, her planning expression falling over her face. She was likely already working through the details of cleaning the cottage for their new neighbors. "Should we invite the family to dine? To welcome them to the neighborhood?"

Mac twisted in his seat again, the reins slack in his hand as the horse continued to pull them along the familiar lane. "It is not a family, but one man and his son, who left the area some twenty years ago. From what I've heard, they have something of a reputation."

"A reputation for what?" Mabel's concerned tone deepened slightly, betraying her worry.

Mac glanced to his children, his gaze sliding past Pippa before he shifted forward again. "We best discuss it later."

"I am not a child," Pippa reminded him. If these men had a reputation, she ought to know about it. From her short conversation with William the day before, she hadn't been able to take his measure, though there was something about the sparkle in his eye and his sly smile that had given her pause. She would certainly avoid the man if he was proven dangerous.

"You may not be a child," Mabel said. She pointed to Elinor and James. "But they are."

James pouted. "I'm a young man." He puffed up his ten-year-old chest. "I should be warned of danger, too."

"We do not know if they are dangerous," Mac said, most likely regretting mentioning anything at all. "We know nothing but rumors of the past, and rumors are not reliable information."

"We can be welcoming if we see them at church," Mabel said. "I do not think we ought to approach anyone with preconceived opinions."

Pippa's gaze fell to the road behind them and the fork in the distance. She waited for a carriage or cart or even a lone rider to turn onto the road and follow them toward the church, but the lane remained sorrowfully empty.

"If they are as bad as you think, I suppose we shan't be seeing them in church," Pippa mused, disappointed.

Mac grunted. "I won't do them the dishonor of making up my mind yet but given the reputation Mr. Blakemore held when he lived here previously, I would caution you all to be mindful."

Mr. Blakemore. So the older man she'd seen shouting orders had been William's father. But who was the blond? A servant? A friend? She'd been a fair distance away, but he hadn't appeared to resemble either of the Blakemore men in the least.

The cart grew silent as they pulled into the churchyard. Mac jumped down from his seat and came around to help Mabel and Pippa before James and Elinor climbed to the ground.

Pippa's curiosity was only growing, fed and watered by Mac's insistent caution. She appreciated his attempt to remain fair, but she could see in the worry lacing her brother-in-law's brow that he was more concerned than he let on.

The Burke family stepped into the churchyard and Pippa broke away from her family to approach Lily. "Tommy is still unwell?" she asked, sweeping her gaze over the family and finding the ten-year-old boy absent.

Lily's freckled complexion wrinkled in worry. "Yes. Mama stayed home with him."

"James will be sad to hear it."

Their families both went toward the church, and Mabel cast a look over her shoulder at Pippa. "We should go inside before we are late."

Pippa stepped forward, lowering her voice as she walked beside her friend toward the old stone building. "We have new neighbors."

"Men?" Lily asked immediately, her eyes shining with hope. There were so few men in Collacott that weren't married, and lately it seemed that most who weren't spent the majority of their day in the tavern.

Pippa couldn't contain her grin. "Handsome men, in fact. But according to Mac, we ought to be wary of the Blakemores."

Lily's face fell. "They've moved into Ravenwood Cottage? You're certain it's them?"

She nodded. "It is a fitting name for that crumbling hovel."

Lily widened her eyes. "Yes, and there is a reason Mr. Blakemore has earned the name Black Heart Blakemore. We ought to stay clear. *Very* clear." Lily had lived her entire life in Collacott, and knew the people's history well. She was wise despite her young age of eighteen, with a balanced head on her shoulders. Her opinion was one to trust.

Disappointment filled Pippa with lead, anchoring her body in place. She followed her friend to the church with heavy steps and turned when she reached the door, surprised to find three riders approaching on horseback.

The riders drew closer, and Pippa sucked in a quiet gasp when she locked eyes with William. His clothes were nicer than his working attire of yesterday—though she'd appreciated the look of the man in his shirtsleeves—and he lifted his black hat toward her, grinning broadly atop his horse. She was overcome with questions and the need to find answers. Why was a man who could afford to outfit himself so nicely for church living in an old, abandoned cottage? Why was his father labeled Black Heart Blakemore? Why did William seem to enjoy bringing a blush to Pippa's cheeks?

The two men beside William didn't appear to notice the quick greeting he had sent her way, and Pippa spun away to enter the church, but not before a wide smile stole over her lips. She tempered it before sitting on the dark wooden bench beside little Elinor.

A murmur swept through the congregation a few short minutes later, and Pippa remained stiffly facing forward, using every minuscule amount of control she possessed to keep from turning to look at the Blakemores' entrance. They were dark-haired and dangerous-looking men, and despite the mild warning Mac and Lily had both cautioned, Pippa found herself interested to learn more about William.

She looked up to find Mabel watching her shrewdly. "You're acting strangely," she whispered, leaning over Elinor.

"I am not."

Mabel's eyes narrowed.

Mr. Robinson rose on the shallow steps up to the raised pulpit and began his sermon by welcoming the people of Colla-cott. But despite his enthusiastic preaching on the merits of turning the other cheek, he failed to hold Pippa's attention. She felt the weight of William's presence somewhere behind her, and it was with great fortitude that she passed the entirety of the church service without so much as turning her head to find him.

CHAPTER 4

$\mathcal{W}$illiam was surprised he hadn't caught Pippa's hair on fire with how fiercely he'd stared at the back of her head during the sprightly vicar's sermon. He willed her to turn around and look at him again, for no other reason than to settle a curiosity he'd developed. Were her eyes blue or dark brown?

When the service came to a close and the vicar made his way to the back of the church to greet parishioners as they exited the building, a sudden, overwhelming desire to be anywhere but Collacott pressed on William like a millstone around his neck. His father nudged him in the back with the head of his cane, the lion-shaped metal digging into him until he stepped out of its reach.

But the message had been imprinted on him clearly: it was time to win over the good people of Collacott.

"As I live and breathe," a man said, approaching them slowly, his eyes crinkling happily. He clapped Father on the back, his floppy white hair moving with each jolly step. "Black Heart Blakemore, himself."

Father's grin spread slowly over his face. It was a guarded

expression, and William was unsure if his father had appreciated the reference. It *had* to be an older reference, for William had never before heard it in his life.

"It has been a long time since I've seen you, John. How is your family?"

That sobered the gentleman. He puffed up his ruddy cheeks and blew out a long breath. "Judith has been better. Hannah is married and lives in Melbury now, so we seldom see her. My nephew is staying with us now instead. Helps out with the fish." He played with the brim in his hand, turning the hat slowly. "Things have been better, but we get by."

Father cuffed his friend John on the shoulder, squeezing. "I've returned, John. You know what that means."

John shook his head, smiling. He lowered his voice. "It means we must be wary of moonless nights and old Donewell Tunnel."

"No," Father said, his smile back in place. "I've returned an injured man." He lifted his cane in a good show for anyone nearby who happened to be listening. "I must rely on the charity of my son now."

"Ah, 'tis a blessed thing, that. Donewell Tunnel has caved in."

The vicar appeared, having foregone his place at the door. His smile was bright, his young face rounded in interest. "Mr. Caney, would you care to introduce me to your friend?"

Mr. John Caney introduced the Blakemores to the vicar, and Father proceeded to present Roger as his cousin's son, giving his surname as Blakemore as well. Perhaps he was *somewhat* aware of the danger Roger faced, or he would have revealed his real surname.

Mr. Robinson, the vicar, was jovial in his effusive greeting. "We love new neighbors in this town."

"I am not exactly a new neighbor," Father said, clapping John Caney on the back as his friend walked away. "My grandfather built the cottage I'm setting up a home in, and three more generations of Blakemores were raised in that house."

"What is with everyone calling that place a *house?*" Roger said quietly. "It's not meant for more than a pair of children. *Such* low ceilings."

William fought a smile. Roger was taller than most men, but even William had to bend down to step through doorways in their cottage. He'd heard his friend bump his head on more than one occasion, only furthering Roger's dislike of Ravenwood Cottage.

William's gaze strayed from the men speaking of Collacott's growth in the last twenty years and found its way toward Pippa and the group she'd sat with—presumably her family—as they made their way outside. Pippa trailed behind two children, a young woman with golden-brown hair wearing a drab, brown dress at her side, speaking rapidly.

"We are in need of a cook," Father said, dragging William's attention away from the now-empty doorway. He wanted to slip outside and greet Pippa, but he knew ingratiating their party with the local clergyman was high on his father's priority list. "Just someone to cook for us once a day or so. Nothing too involved."

"I do know of a young woman who would be glad of the position," Mr. Robinson said thoughtfully. He rubbed his clean-shaven chin. "Lily Burke has always had an affinity for cooking, and I'm certain she would not disappoint. I tasted a blackberry muffin of hers the other day, and it was heavenly."

"Burke," Father said, rolling the name on his tongue. His gaze searched the remaining parishioners but didn't settle on anyone in particular. "Would you be so good as to introduce us?"

Mr. Robinson led them outside. The sun had risen higher during the sermon, burning off the dregs of cold that had clung to the morning air. People grouped in the vast churchyard, and friendly, whispered conversations rose in volume as the Blakemores walked through their ranks. William felt eyes on him from every angle, and while he was used to some attention, such a sheer amount of focus was unnerving.

"Mr. Burke," the vicar said to a man in a worn, brown coat and hat that had seen too many years. "Allow me the pleasure to introduce—"

"No need," Mr. Burke said, stepping away from the small group he'd been chatting with. He had weather-beaten skin that was old and leathered much like Father's and appeared to be similar in age. He pulled his hat from his head, revealing light brown hair that thinned over his crown. "It's been a long time, Richard."

"Too long. I meant to make it back here before now, but things never quite slowed down before now." Father reached back and clasped William on the arm, and he stepped forward. "This is my son."

Mr. Burke eyed William closely. He swallowed hard and his throat bobbed, and he seemed to shake himself. "He looks like you, Richard." He smiled. "Unfortunate fellow."

That pulled a smile from William's tight chest. He'd known that this was the land his father had grown up in. Indeed, William had spent the first five years of his life here as well, though he hardly remembered them. They'd moved on to Dorset when he was still young enough to forget most things about his childhood; only the snatches of warm evenings by the fire and his mother's sweet voice rested in the murky cobwebs in his mind.

"That is where the resemblance ends," Father said. "He's more Cecilia than me, God rest her soul."

Mr. Burke froze, his body tensing on the impact of those words. Had he known William's mother, too? The news of her death appeared to be something of a shock, though it had occurred nearly five years before.

"Edith will be sad to hear it."

"Where is Edith?"

Mr. Burke's gaze strayed toward Pippa's family, and William fought the temptation to follow it there. "Home with my youngest, Tommy. He's unwell. It's a mere cold, but he's possessed of a sickly constitution."

"I've been told you have a daughter who might be willing to cook for us," Father said, wasting no time. He cracked a smile. "My son and my cousin and I, that is. If we are left to our own devices, we'll be eating stew every day, and not a pleasant one at that."

Mr. Burke looked again to Pippa's family, his eyes narrowing. "I'll have to ask my Lily, but she's a fine cook. Her stew would be pleasant enough, and you'll have bread to go with it, no doubt."

"It sounds to be an improvement already."

Mr. Burke smiled. "Come, I'll introduce you."

He led them across the open lawn toward Pippa and the group she was speaking to. Her gaze lifted, snagging on him, and William sent her a brief smile. Pink bloomed on her tanned cheeks, and she looked away.

"Lily, I want you to meet an old friend of mine," Mr. Burke said.

The young woman who'd been speaking to Pippa since the end of the sermon stepped forward, her pale green eyes rounding in interest as she came to rest beside her father. She dipped in a curtsy as the introductions were made, but her gaze kept straying back to William.

He swallowed a sigh. It was of no interest to him to employ a cook who would watch him with such unabashed curiosity. Perhaps he could do his best later that evening to make a stew worth eating and put Father off the idea of hiring anyone at all.

"How long do you plan to remain in Collacott?" Mr. Burke asked, the unspoken question lingering on the edges of his nervous words. He likely wanted to know if the Blakemores' presence was a threat at all. To his fishing, to his safety, to his daughter . . . only on the last thing could William safely promise he would not interfere.

Once the smuggling had begun, no one was safe.

No one.

"That depends on how long I can convince my boy to stay with me," Father said, affecting affection that was more parts false than not. He clapped William on the back and infused his voice with a warmth that William seldom heard. "I hope a good, long while, but one cannot control their grown sons, of course. I hope we remain here for good."

No, one could not typically control their grown sons, but Father somehow had. He wielded guilt like a well-trained hound and maintained control over the leash that bound William, despite their differing opinions. To claim his intent to remain in Collacott for good, though? That was doing it much too brown.

"How fortunate for us," Mr. Burke said. "Come, meet your neighbors." He indicated a tall, broad man behind him, and gestured the gentleman forward. A woman followed close to his side, holding a chubby, cherry-cheeked babe. Pippa edged in close to the woman as the children they'd sat with ran off to play with their friends.

"Mr. MacKenzie," Mr. Burke began.

"But everyone calls me Mac," the giant said, cutting in with a pleasant smile, the easy expression of a man comfortable in his own boots. "This is my wife, Mrs. MacKenzie, our son Liam, and my sister-in-law, Miss Sheffield. Our other two are running about somewhere."

"Getting into trouble, most likely," Mrs. Mackenzie said wryly, dipping a curtsy.

Father gestured to him. "This is my son, Mr. William Blakemore, and my cousin's son, Mr. Roger Blakemore."

Bows and curtsies were exchanged without missing a beat,

and Roger hung back a little, allowing Father to make the connection with no argument. His quiet acceptance grated on William, for though he had no choice but to heed his father's wishes, Roger was a free man and could do as he wanted.

"We would love to have you over to dine, Mr. Blakemore," Mrs. Mackenzie said. He could sense a hesitancy to her words, and she turned to include the Burkes in her invitation. "You know we would be happy if both of your families would join us. We can wait to plan a day when Tommy is better and Edith won't need to remain home with him."

Mr. Burke began to put her off. "Oh, I'm not sure—"

"We should enjoy that very much," Father said. He speared Burke with a look. "I haven't seen my good friends in twenty years, at least. A reunion is certainly in order."

"It is settled," Mrs. Mackenzie said. A victorious look shone in her dark blue eyes.

Pippa slipped up beside her friend and strung her arm through Lily's. She whispered something so close to Lily's ear that the hair moved on the side of her face, and William wished he could know what was being said. Lily nodded softly.

"It was a pleasure to meet you," Pippa said, curtsying as she pulled her friend away. "Welcome back to Collacott."

"Pippa, you certainly do not mean to walk," Mrs. Mackenzie said.

Dragging her friend away, Pippa lifted her chin. "I intend to do just that."

Mrs. Mackenzie shook her head slightly but didn't argue further. Though William believed he heard her mutter, "It's your cold dinner, then."

Father must have been too long on his feet, for his expression grew tight. "Send word when you have an answer," he said to Mr. Burke, before begging his excuses and turning toward where they'd left their horses. William helped Father onto his horse before mounting his own and pulling it in line behind

Roger. They waved to the few people they'd met, and William bit back his regret at not being more forward. Father had asked him to spread his charm, and he'd done very little of that.

Pippa had distracted him. They pulled onto the road that led toward home and off to the side of the lane as they passed Pippa walking with Lily.

Once they were out of earshot, Father pulled his horse beside William's. Pain was written into the contortion of his expression and the lines on his face, but he was a stubborn man, and he would ride until he could no longer get into the saddle on his own. "I want you to try harder next time."

William nodded, his jaw set. He'd known his own failings, knew how he'd been a disappointment. "I will."

"Maybe that Sheffield girl would be a good target."

Target. The word soured his stomach. He clenched his teeth and did not bother to hide his distaste. "I will target no one in that way. I never have, and I do not intend to begin now."

"But if you only—"

"I am willing to befriend the entire town, Father, but I will not lead a woman to believe that I harbor feelings where none reside."

"Flirting has never been about *feelings*," Roger said, laughing to himself.

Which was where he and William differed. There was a stark difference between playful banter and choosing a woman to direct his affections to.

He looked over his shoulder and caught sight of Pippa in the distance, walking beside her friend. She looked innocent and happy, and William wondered what it was about this woman that had captured his attention.

And what, exactly, had captured his father's notice, too?

CHAPTER 5

*P*ippa watched the Blakemore men ride out of sight, her gaze snagging on William as he looked at her over his shoulder.

"That is a fine-looking gentleman," Lily said under her breath. "I about lost my ability to speak in his presence."

"He's just a man, Lily."

"No, he was more than that," she said reverently. "He was Adonis himself."

Good grief, the woman was leaning dangerously close to worship. William was excessively handsome with his brooding eyes and his square jaw, but he was not godlike. There was too much mischief lurking in his gaze for such an attribute.

Lily sighed wistfully. "Do you think a gentleman like him would ever notice someone like me? He looked so noble."

"Of course he would notice you, Lily. You are beautiful and possessed of a radiant smile." Pippa was alarmingly tempted to take her friend by the shoulders and shake sense into her. Lily's worth was greater than the acceptance or dismissal of any gentleman, regardless of Society's opinions on the matter. "But whether or not you should *want* a cad to notice you is more to the point."

"How do you know he is a cad?"

Pippa's tongue grew thick. She hadn't mentioned her meeting in the woods to anyone. Surely any man who would flirt so blatantly was a cad, was he not? But it did not paint her in a good light to have been caught spying on her new neighbor, and no one else would believe the story that she'd been looking for a bird. She wasn't entirely convinced William had even believed it.

But more than that, she did not wish to share that little adventure with anyone else, not even Lily. She wouldn't examine the reasons for that now.

"I suppose I don't know if he is a cad or not, I merely made an assumption. Though I would wager that my assessment is not far off the mark."

"You cannot know that yet," Lily scolded. "Do not assign negative traits where they've yet to be proven."

Pippa blinked at her friend. "Was it not you who warned me away from Black Heart Blakemore just this morning?"

Lily stopped in the center of the lane, her arm slipping free of Pippa's and her nose wrinkling in thought. Her bonnet shaded her eyes from the sun, but light shone on the golden-brown hair peeking out the back. "I suppose I did warn you away from them, didn't I? My father is wary of their return." Her eyebrows bunched. "Though he seemed perfectly at ease with the Blakemores in the churchyard, did he not? They spoke together comfortably. It seems as though he is no longer worried."

"You would need to ask him that. I'm not sure."

Lily seemed to contemplate this for a moment. The rushing of waves splashing against the cliff they walked along punctuated the silence as wind whipped their skirts about their legs. "Perhaps we ought to wait until we know the

Blakemores better before we make up our minds about them."

"Perhaps a handsome face has caused you to recant your warning, you mean?" Pippa asked, grinning.

A blush stole up Lily's neck, and she laughed, though she did not deny the claim. A handsome face, indeed. There were more than enough handsome faces to go around all of England. The trouble was that most of them lacked much of anything behind their attractive facade.

A handsome face meant nothing to Pippa if there was no brain behind it.

Wheels on the hard-packed earth rolled behind them, and the women stepped off the lane to allow the carriage to pass, waving to the family they knew inside.

"There are so few men in Collacott, Pip," Lily said. "Not all of us can go off to London to secure a match."

Pippa felt the sting of her friend's words wrapped in guilt. She'd had a chance when her sister had taken her to London for the Season earlier that year, but it had been an utter waste. Even though Pippa had intentionally refrained from informing anyone about her large dowry, there were men aplenty who'd asked her to dance or brought her flowers and begged a quarter-hour of her time. But none of them had been the least bit interesting.

She would not marry for the sake of gaining a husband. She would only marry for love.

Still, Lily made a valid point. Collacott boasted very few men. The Blakemores had no idea what sort of situation they'd soon find themselves in. Surely every eligible young woman would be knocking at their cottage door within the week—small and discreet as it was.

"I shouldn't put on airs," Lily said at length. "I'm more suited to sew the man's clothes than I am to dance with him. It would be much better to set my sights on a reasonable objective than to be disappointed."

Pippa stopped walking and tugged her friend to a halt. Irritation reared its head within her, warring with the understanding that Lily *was* a lower station than the Blakemores seemed to be. But that shouldn't matter, and Pippa hated that it did, that Lily's concerns were valid. She wished she had the power to change it. Lily was worth far more than her station allotted her.

Looking her in the eye, Pippa spoke with quiet conviction. "You are worth a hundred, no, a *thousand* William Blakemores, and you certainly do not need to temper your aspirations."

Lily smiled gently. "You are too kind to me, Pip." She gave Pippa the sort of look one casts upon their cat as it delivers a mouse at one's feet. It was an excellent effort, but not entirely appreciated.

They moved to the side of the lane as another cart approached. "Lily," Mr. Burke called from his driver's seat. He tugged the reins and slowed his horse. "We should be getting home now."

Lily pulled Pippa in for a hug. "You are the dearest of friends."

"You only think that because you cannot be friends with yourself," Pippa said.

"Shall we go down to the cove tomorrow?" Lily asked, moving to the driver's seat to climb up and sit beside her papa.

"You'll be busy tomorrow," Mr. Burke said, lifting his light brown eyebrows. "Mr. Blakemore himself is looking for a cook, and the vicar directed him our way."

"Me?" Lily asked, her eyes rounding wide like saucers. "I've not cooked for another household before."

"It's only the three men," Mr. Burke said. "I'll wager anything you present to them will be an improvement."

Pippa could see the ideas churning in Lily's mind, her gaze far away.

"Do you not think that is unsafe?" Pippa asked, gathering Mr. Burke's attention and Lily's quick scowl. "What do we know of these men? They've been gone for two decades and from what I've heard, their reputations weren't above reproach before they left."

Mr. Burke lifted his hat and scratched the top of his head. "Lily will be safe enough. The danger Richard poses has nothing to do with his kitchen." He paused. "Or, it shouldn't, at least. No, as long as Lily is home before dark, all will be well."

The unspoken addition to his sentiments hung thick in the air between them, swirling about by the gusts blowing off the coast. The Burkes could use the money badly, and Lily *was* an excellent cook. She'd learned from her mama, the best in all of Collacott, in Pippa's humble opinion.

"I begin tomorrow?" Lily asked.

Her father nodded.

She looked much too excited for a woman who had moments before professed the need to realign where she set her *sights.* It would appear that Lily's heart could not be so easily dissuaded from the prospect of a handsome man.

The sound of Mac's cart rumbled toward them, and Mr. Burke lifted the reins and slapped them down again, urging his horse forward. He lifted his hand in a wave behind him as Lily grinned. "I'll come see you soon so I can tell you everything!"

Pippa waved them farewell and stepped back to approach her sister.

"Would you like to ride the rest of the way home with us?" Mabel asked.

"No, I think I will walk along the beach while the weather is so mild."

Mabel didn't look pleased, but Mac sent Pippa an easy smile. "We'll come fetch you from the cove if we need you."

"I shouldn't be too long," Pippa said, straining against the frustration that Mabel felt the need to keep track of where she meant to be. She understood that Mabel was doing her best to care for Pippa's safety, but could she not trust a little more?

Pippa wasn't a child anymore. "And I won't go beyond the cove."

Mac appeared satisfied with this.

"I want to come!" James said. "May I, Auntie?"

"Of course—if your mama permits it."

"Me too, please," Elinor said.

Mabel looked as though she was going to argue, but she relented, making her children promise not to soil their Sunday clothes. James and Elinor both jumped down from the back of the cart. They waved their parents and baby brother farewell and walked alongside Pippa as they followed the cliffside lane toward home. The cart holding the rest of their family continued down the road until it disappeared from sight.

They took their time reaching the cove, pausing to gather the few remaining daisy-like yellow ragworts as they went. When they neared the path that led down to the small beach, James ran ahead, skipping away with unabashed glee. Elinor sedately picked the yellow petals from her sad, drooping flowers and dropped them into the wind, watching them fly away one by one and litter the pathway.

"Do you think if I find a kitten, Mama will let me keep it?"

Pippa looked about her at the wide, open beach and rocky cliffside. Where Elinor planned to find this kitten was a mystery. "You would have to ask her, but I would assume they could always use more kittens in the stables."

Elinor bunched her little nose. "No, not the stables. I would want my kitten to live in the nursery with me. There is plenty of room in my bed."

"I'm sure there is, and you are so kind to wish to share your room." They reached the beach, and Elinor ran after her brother, who was climbing his way along the rock pools in search of small animals. Pippa untied her bonnet and let it dangle from her hand by the ribbons. She lifted her face to the sun, closing her eyes and breathing in the salty air.

James's laughter broke through her reverie, and she breathed out, following her niece and nephew toward the shallow rock pools on the side of the cove.

Just past the pools where the sea began in earnest sat an outcrop protruding from the edge of the cove. The tide was low enough to reach the base of the rocks, and Pippa had been considering climbing it for some time, but she couldn't do so in front of her niece and nephew. Mabel had spoken to her on more than one occasion about setting a good example for them, and apparently climbing trees and rocks in a dress was not proper behavior for anyone, let alone a young lady.

Which only showed how much Mabel had changed. She'd never forbidden Pippa from climbing trees in her childhood. If she had, Pippa couldn't recall it. And Pippa had turned out to be a lovely adult, hadn't she? It wasn't her fault that she ended up in scrapes more often than not. She had an adventurous spirit.

"Auntie! A crab!" James looked up from where he squatted a few yards away and Pippa hurried toward him, picking her way over the dryer rocks.

"Don't dirty your Sunday clothes or your mother will be furious with me," Pippa said as Elinor rushed to hide behind her.

James hadn't seemed to hear her. He lifted the crab from the water, grinning as he raised it high above the rocks. "Come see it, Elinor."

"No," she said, staying behind Pippa and peeking out at her brother. "You'll toss it at me."

"Will not."

"Will too."

Pippa's balance wavered, and she reached back to steady her niece and keep them both from falling into the cold water. "James will not throw the crab at you, because he is a *kind* brother, and he doesn't wish to *distress* you." She emphasized her words, sending a wide-eyed look to her nephew.

"I promise!" James called.

Elinor tentatively stepped out from behind Pippa's skirt, and James raised the crab to show her. Once she got close enough to see the animal, its legs and claws squirming mid-air, James jerked it forward, pretending to toss it at his sister, though it never left his hands.

Elinor screamed. She backed up, losing her footing, and slipping on the wet rocks. She splashed in the shallow pools, her high-pitched shriek renting the air unabated.

Oh, drat. Her dress. Mabel was going to be vexed.

Pippa sent James a scowl, and he tucked back into himself, his cheeks pinking under her scrutiny. "I didn't mean to make her fall," he said defensively. "I only wanted to scare her."

Pippa stepped closer to her distraught niece. "Elinor, have you hurt—*Elinor*, I cannot speak to you when you wail on so. Hush a moment, darling."

Elinor was far too busy screaming to hear Pippa's plea, and she continued to cry, lying on her side in the shallow water as it rose and lowered slightly with the tide. Elinor's light brown hair was strewn beside her in the water and tears streaked her cheeks.

"Someone is coming," James said, pointing behind Pippa.

She turned to see a man running down the steep, sloped pathway to the beach, removing his coat as he went. A ball of unease lodged in Pippa's throat, drying her voice as she watched William Blakemore toss his Sunday coat—or she assumed that is what it was, for it was well-made and cut close to his figure—into the dirty sand and run across the rocky beach. She stared at him as though he were a crab with two heads.

Pippa didn't have the heart to tell the man hastening to Elinor's rescue that the little girl was prone to theatrics and not likely injured. He had real fear in his eyes, which was understandable. Elinor's screams *did* sound awfully loud.

"What happened?" he called as he neared, his chest heaving,

breath panting. He reached up to loosen his cravat and revealed a tanned triangle of skin.

Pippa forced her gaze away from his neck.

"Is she hurt?"

Pippa crouched down and gently took Elinor by the hand. The surprise of a man appearing out of nowhere must have subdued her, for her crying had slowed to silent, whining sobs. "Elinor, are you hurt?"

Elinor nodded, her bottom lip pushed out as she lay in the freezing water. But was she nodding because of her injured pride, or had she truly hurt herself in her fall? It was difficult to know when to take her seriously, and she appeared well enough.

"Come. Let us get you home," Pippa said, eager for something to do that might remove the image of William running to rescue them from her mind. It was no use. He'd been seared into her thoughts, appearing in his haste over and over again without any prompting on Pippa's part.

He'd looked like such a hero, and that was a handsome quality in a man.

Elinor continued to sob quietly as she allowed Pippa to help her stand. William splashed through the rock pools, seemingly heedless of the water drenching his boots and pantaloons. "I can carry her." He gestured as though he meant to lift Elinor in his arms. "Shall I take you home, little one?"

Elinor gazed up at her savior in admiration, and Pippa smarted. She'd been right beside her niece the entire time yet was allotted none of Elinor's grave gratitude. Quite unfair.

"You really needn't go to such trouble," Pippa said. "Elinor can probably walk. Can you not, Ellie?"

Elinor shook her head. Pippa refrained from rolling her eyes. Even her niece was struck by this man.

William glanced at Pippa, his blue eyes steady and far too close. She reminded herself to breathe. Perhaps she'd been too hard on Lily earlier. The woman was *somewhat* justified in her quick change of opinion regarding their new neighbor. But Pippa wouldn't allow herself to fall into his trap. A man who would flirt so frivolously with a woman he'd only just met was *not* the sort of man for her.

Pippa, embarrassingly enough, had been quite stricken herself when she'd first laid eyes on the gentleman. But time and space had reminded her of the importance of knowing a man's heart. She could stay strong in the face of such handsomeness.

"I didn't mean to make her fall," James said again, the squirming crab still in his grip. "I only wished to frighten her."

"Of course you didn't intend for her to fall." William looked up from where he crouched beside Elinor. "It is a brother's duty to cause havoc, and a sister's duty to retaliate." He turned his attention to Elinor. "Perhaps with a frog later in his best shoes?"

"There will be no frogs in anyone's shoes," Pippa said sternly. She sounded exactly like Mabel, and the realization of that gave her pause.

William lowered his voice. "We'll plan our attack when your aunt is otherwise occupied, eh?"

Elinor gave a watery giggle, nodding up at William, and James laughed, though it was his shoes whose demise was being plotted. William lifted Elinor in his arms easily and turned for the beach.

"Leave the crab," Pippa said when James moved to follow them.

He frowned, setting the crab back on the slick rocks, and it scurried sideways until it found a pool to hide in.

"Will you direct me toward your house?" William asked, and Elinor nodded in his arms.

James ran ahead of him toward the foot of the path up the hill. "I can show you the way to go."

"I know how to direct him home, James!" Elinor argued. "I am the one he asked."

James glanced back at his sister and paused, very likely weighing his guilt with the desire to lead their procession. "Very well." He allowed William to pass and followed close behind them.

Pippa crossed the beach to retrieve William's coat. She draped it over her arm and lifted the hem of her skirt to climb the sloping pathway to the top of the rise. Camden Court wasn't too far from the cove, which was how they shared a name. Though William didn't appear tired from this distance, she imagined it wouldn't be easy to carry Elinor too far.

William and James waited for Pippa at the top of the rise, standing on the cliffside and looking out over the sea. Her breathing was labored from the climb, and she caught William looking at the coat in her arms.

"Thank you," he said.

She was taken aback by the polite gratitude in his tone. "Of course. You are carrying something precious to me. I didn't wish to leave your coat at the mercy of the—"

"Birds?"

"I intended to say wind, but yes, I suppose the birds were something of a danger as well."

His eyes sparkled as he turned down the lane toward Camden Court, following James. Pippa fell in step beside him.

"Those birds. Such troublesome creatures." He glanced at her sideways, his voice deceptively innocent. "Tell me, why were you chasing birds again? Are you a student of ornithology?"

Heat bled up Pippa's neck, and she averted her gaze. He was referring to her flimsy excuse for climbing the tree near his cottage.

"Pippa wasn't chasing birds," Elinor said matter-of-factly between quiet sobs. "She was protecting your coat from them."

"Ah, of course," he said, as though he'd misunderstood. He shot Pippa a brief conspiratorial look, and she fought down the rising tide of warmth in her chest.

Oh, good heavens. She hadn't survived an entire Season of handsome men giving her attention with her heart intact to now fall victim to the charms of a charismatic fop.

Well, he wasn't a fop. He simply looked good in everything he wore.

Sweeping past William, Elinor, and James, Pippa crossed through the tree-lined entry to Camden Court and straight toward the stone house, ignoring the pleasant feel of William's eyes on her back.

CHAPTER 6

*T*he tree-lined drive dripped with foliage that rose and hung over the shady lane. William's boots stomped through the short gravel drive that led up to the dark stone house. It was a decently sized home, not so large as to be pretentious, but beautiful all the same with its dark green moss growing over the gray stone. William enjoyed the setting of his grandfather's cottage, small as it might be, but it was drafty and dark. This house, however, looked nothing short of perfect.

It was far removed from the clean lines and stark whiteness of the Palladian house William had resided in for the last twenty years, but perhaps that was part of the appeal.

"Bring her this way," Pippa said, gesturing toward the large front door. She opened it and stepped aside. William caught a whiff of something floral when he passed Pippa and wanted to slow his steps, to breathe a little deeper, but he continued to follow James down the corridor and into a small sitting room.

Dampness had seeped through his waistcoat and dripped down the front of his pantaloons, chilling his skin. The girl had dripped most of the way home, and William seemed to have absorbed a good amount of the seawater. Elinor's renewed cries shook her little body upon reaching her home, though William assumed she was more offended by her brother's antics than hurt.

The door closed, and Pippa's footsteps were close behind him. He couldn't decipher exactly what it was about the woman that had caught his attention, but she had successfully snared him like a fish on a hook. He wanted to stroll beside her and ask her to tell him more about herself. How was this young woman who looked so prim and proper in her bonnet and shawl, sitting straight-backed in the church pew, her attention riveted by the vicar so deeply that she hardly looked elsewhere over the duration of the sermon, the same young woman who chose to walk home from church, to remove her bonnet and shamelessly allow the sun to tan her cheeks, and who climbed trees when no one else was nearby?

Pippa was a puzzle, and William was awfully fond of deciphering puzzles.

"Elinor is well, though a trifle wet," Pippa said immediately when her older sister stood from the sofa, the babe in her arms squirming to see who had just entered the room. "She was startled and fell in the rock pools."

Pippa laid William's coat over the back of a chair and set down her bonnet before taking the small babe from her sister. Mrs. Mackenzie came to stand before William, giving him a curious yet grateful look. "And you happened upon them? You must accept my gratitude for carrying Elinor all the way home."

William handed the child to her mother. He smiled down at Elinor's little face before she calmly buried it in her mother's neck, holding her tiny hands to her chest. "It was her . . . distress . . . that alerted me to the trouble. How could I not run to the aid of a young woman whose cries carried to me all the way on the cliffside?"

And run, he had. William had been frightened upon hearing the screams, the sound transporting him back in time to that awful day five years earlier that had forever changed his life. William hadn't hesitated even a moment. The sound of young Elinor's distress was a sudden ignitor within him, spurning him into immediate action like a flame to kindling.

Mrs. Mackenzie's lips twitched. "Still, I thank you all the same. Please tell me you'll stay for some tea."

William's gaze sought Pippa. She looked away quickly, and he wickedly wished to drive *her* into action. He didn't appreciate this polite, prim Pippa as much as he did the witty, snappy one.

His shirt stuck to his stomach though, the dampness on the front of his legs from carrying Elinor making him appear a mess. "If I was the least bit presentable, I would love to accept your offer. As it stands, I'm afraid I'm not fit for company."

"Oh, dear. Elinor did that, did she not?" Mrs. Mackenzie asked, locating the dampness on his waistcoat and shirt sleeves with her eyes. She clicked her tongue. "Now I really must insist that you remain. We are not so stuffy as to refuse a damp gentleman a much-needed restorative cup of tea." She moved toward the door, then paused and looked back at him. "I'll send for some cake, too. I'm certain you must be famished after carrying Elinor all the way home."

William was used to carrying barrels of brandy up steep climbs in the dark that weighed more than that little slip of a girl. The walk hadn't been a trial in the least. But he certainly would never refuse cake.

"After the sorry fare I've been subject to the last few days, cake certainly sounds marvelous."

Mrs. Mackenzie indicated where William could sit. "I'm going to take Elinor up to change into dry clothing, but I'll return quickly." She looked from the open doorway to her son. "James, you will remain until I return?"

"Of course, Mama."

She smiled before quitting the room with her distraught young daughter in her arms.

"Mama told us that your cottage has been empty for longer than I've been alive," James said. The young boy had wide, curious eyes that made it difficult for William to look away.

Pippa walked toward the window, bouncing the baby in her arms, and William moved to sit on the edge of a ladder-back, wooden chair near James. If he were to leave a wet smudge behind on this seat, it would hardly suffer. "My father lived his whole life in that cottage, but I only lived there until I was five, so I hardly remember anything about it. And your mother is correct. When we left it, no one moved in to take our place and our house has been empty ever since."

"Our house was empty before my papa and mama were married, too," James said. "Now it is so full, we hardly have room for all of us."

William understood that sentiment well. His cottage had two cramped bedchambers, one on the ground floor and the second upstairs. Due to his immobility, Father had taken the downstairs chamber, leaving William to share his space with Roger. They were friends, of course, and had worked together for nearly a decade now, but one could only manage being around the same man day in and out for so long. William was certain he would go mad if he were forced to remain in Roger's company forevermore. The little walks he'd begun taking alone had helped to clear his mind and give him a break from his overfilled house.

Today, his walk had been exceedingly beneficial as it had led to this little interlude. Tea and cake, which he was massively looking forward to, and Pippa.

Pippa crossed toward him and James, lifting the coat from where it rested on the back of a chair and bringing it to William. He accepted it, brushing her fingers, and he wished they didn't have gloves layered between them. He wondered if her skin was smooth or rough. Given the size of her home and the two servants he'd already seen, he would typically assume her skin to be as smooth as the porcelain teacup he would soon be drinking from. But Pippa wasn't like anyone else he knew. She climbed trees and walked in rockpools. Did that roughen her skin?

Curiosity pulsed within him, crowded by the hollow emptiness of his stomach. A rumble rolled loudly.

Pippa sat on the sofa opposite him, bouncing the baby on her knee. She looked to his stomach, where the sound had emanated from, no doubt having heard it. "I'm told that you are looking to hire a cook."

Yes. She'd definitely heard it. How embarrassing.

He lifted an eyebrow, bringing one ankle up to rest on the opposite knee. "Are you offering your services, Miss Sheffield?"

Pippa laughed, her eyebrows drawing together. Her eyes flashed to James before settling on the baby in her lap. It would appear that she did not intend to engage in any degree of flirtation when there was company present. Very well, William could work around that.

He smoothed his coat over his lap. He hadn't yet tightened his cravat, but he'd watched Pippa's eyes dip to his exposed neck more than once, so he felt no great motivation to tighten it yet. "My kitchen would certainly be brighter if you—"

"You do not want my auntie to be your cook," James said, scoffing. "Not unless you only wish to eat muffins."

"Does Miss Sheffield make muffins, then?"

"Yes, and they're quite good," Pippa said primly.

"They are good," James added, "but she makes nothing else."

"I think I could easily subsist on a diet of muffins and nothing else."

"Are you not looking to hire Lily Burke?" she asked. Her voice raised a little, her tone growing higher. Did William detect a hint of alarm in her tone?

"Ah, yes. I believe my father spoke to Mr. Burke today."

The baby whined and Pippa stood, bouncing him on her hip as though it was the most natural thing in the world. "Shhh,

Liam," she crooned. She removed her glove and gave it to him to play with, and he quieted. Returning her attention to William, she smiled. "I am grateful that you thought to ask Miss Burke. She is an excellent cook and will provide you with far more than measly muffins."

At this moment, William did not want anything more. He watched Pippa's bare hand ball into a loose fist, the back of her knuckles stroking her nephew's soft cheek. William's heart constricted, the love in her tender touch so achingly apparent it flooded him with grief over his own loss. He shook himself, hoping to rid the demons that threatened to descend upon him. He couldn't think about Mother's death, about how wholly it had been avoidable, not unless he wanted to be overcome with anger and fury and thrown into a rage.

No, he needed to temper those thoughts and replace them with something, *anything* else.

Squaring his gaze on Pippa, he tried to smirk. "Of course, if you'd like to present me with a muffin—"

"Mr. Blakemore," a booming voice said from the doorway. Mac filled the space, ducking his head to enter the small, cozy sitting room, and crossed the floor. "My wife told me that we had a visitor. I believe I have you to thank for bringing my daughter home from the cove?"

"She likely could have walked well enough on her own," William said, glad his flirtatious remark had been interrupted before he could condemn himself.

Mac's gaze dropped to William's disheveled cravat and absent coat. He crossed his arms, and his imposing height was intimidating. William wasn't one to scare easily, but he hadn't before encountered such a massive, sturdy gentleman.

William swallowed, suddenly filled with motivation to tighten his cravat again.

A maid came into the room with a tray of tea and cake and set it on the small table in the center of the room. Mac moved to sit beside Pippa and took Liam from her arms so she could pour the tea. Mac's monstrous size made the chubby, rosy-cheeked babe look even smaller, but he held Liam in a delicate, gentle way.

"How do you take your tea?" Pippa asked, snapping William's attention to her. He couldn't remember the last time he'd seen a man hold his own baby this way, and it struck him as odd. He respected Mac greater for it, though he couldn't say exactly why that was.

"Sugar and milk, if you have it."

Pippa's eyebrows lifted as she proceeded to pour. He wanted to tease her, to find out how she took her tea—he suspected with heaping amounts of sugar—but Mac's watchful eye made the words die swiftly on his tongue. He accepted the tea with gratitude, drinking the warm liquid and allowing it to soothe his hungry stomach.

He really ought to remember to eat *before* taking a walk next time.

"Mr. Blakemore has hired Lily to cook for his family," Pippa said, pouring and preparing her brother-in-law's tea.

Mac accepted the cup, keeping it out of reach of the baby. "Is that so? She makes an excellent pasty."

William had the distinct feeling that Lily Burke was a close friend to this family.

"No, Liam," Mac said, moving the cup further from his son's reach.

Pippa handed James a cup of tea before preparing her own. She sliced the cake and distributed it on little plates, and William's mouth salivated as the moist pound cake hit his tongue.

Mac peered at William so long he wondered if he'd accidentally loosened his cravat further instead of tightening it. "You'll need to get started on tilling soon if you intend to plant for the spring."

William hadn't thought of that, and he was inordinately glad that the man had farming on his mind. He was large and intimidating and William didn't want him to discern his growing interest in Pippa.

Though, Mac made a valid point. They chose early autumn to arrive at the cottage—well, *chose* wasn't entirely true, as they hadn't had much choice at all in the matter—and it was too late for some of the vegetables he knew they'd need. If they were going to winter in Devonshire, they needed to make a plan. "I hoped to start fishing tomorrow night."

"They've explained the tithes and boundaries?"

"No, but my father intends to take care of that tomorrow. Perhaps I'm better off working the land first."

Mac swallowed another drink of tea before putting his cup down and rearranging Liam on his lap. "Let me see what I can pull together. I'm sure a few local men wouldn't mind helping, and we can get your land ready much faster with a group of us than you can on your own."

"I have my frien—my cousin, Roger, as well." William took another swallow of tea, hoping his mistake hadn't been noticed. "Together I think we can manage. But I will never reject extra help."

"My papa is very strong," James said, nodding to emphasize his words. "He was in the royal navy, so he knows quite a lot about everything. My grandfather, too."

William's gaze flicked to Mac, his heart thudding loudly in his chest. His nearest neighbor was a navy man? That was not good. Not good at all. "Your grandfather too, eh?" he asked, hoping James would freely offer more information.

"Captain Sheffield," James said proudly. "He's in Algiers now, but he visits when he can."

"I'm sure he misses you when he's away," William said, though his mind was whirring faster than a spinning wheel. Did Father know about this connection? Surely the Mackenzies hadn't been at Camden Court long enough to be familiar with his family. "James mentioned that this house was empty before you moved here?" he said, hoping to gather more information.

Mac nodded. "It sat vacant for a few years, but we snapped it up and filled the hearths with fire again. It hasn't been too drafty, despite the sea being so near."

Mrs. Mackenzie came into the small sitting room, her eyebrows drawn in concern. She cast a strained smile at William before settling her attention on her husband. "I fear we ought to send for the doctor."

Pippa set her cup on the table. "Is Elinor truly hurt?"

"She may have broken a bone. I cannot tell, but her arm is tender to the touch and is beginning to swell."

Pippa and Mac stood in unison, Pippa's hand resting on her heart. "Oh, Mabel. I feel terrible. I shouldn't have assumed she was well."

Mrs. Mackenzie shook her head. "You couldn't have known. Mac, will you ride to Dr. Garvey?"

"Straight away."

Mrs. Mackenzie glanced at the tea platter. "Forgive me, Mr. Blakemore. I'm afraid I haven't been the greatest hostess today."

"Pippa has done a fine job of it in your stead," Mac said, taking his wife's hand and squeezing her fingers. He passed Liam into her arms and bent to kiss her on the cheek before striding from the room.

William watched James slip another slice of cake onto his plate when no one was looking. He froze when he caught William's eye, but William winked at the boy, and a guilty, wide smile fell over his face.

Liam whined, and Mrs. Mackenzie bounced him on her hip, her worried gaze resting on the ceiling.

"Give Liam here," Pippa said, approaching with her arms out.

"No, he needs to nap. I'll take him up to Hope. You'll see to our guest?"

Pippa nodded, but William stood. "I believe it is past time I am on my way. Is there anything I can do for you before I leave?"

Mrs. Mackenzie smiled warmly at him. She was a lovely, taller version of Pippa, and William liked her welcoming, affectionate presence.

She reminded him of his own mother, of the way she kept her house running like a tight ship but always had a pleasant smile and a warm biscuit to sneak into his eager hands. He slid the memories away and tucked them into the back of his mind.

"You are most welcome here any time, Mr. Blakemore. I cannot thank you enough for responding to my darling Elinor's shrieking. I'm certain we are fortunate for gaining such a gallant neighbor."

He dipped in a bow, for words seemed to completely flee his dry mouth. Would Mrs. Mackenzie feel so fortunate to learn that William's father planned to bring smuggling to their shores? He swallowed the bile rising in his throat. Most people approved of smuggling, even participated in it, for they appreciated the affordable tea, sugar, and brandy it provided them. But a navy man? Surely this family was the exception.

Pippa walked William to the front door as Mrs. Mackenzie escaped up the stairs and James remained in the sitting room with his third—or fourth, perhaps—slice of cake. A groove lined the space between her brows, and William itched to smooth it away.

"I have never known a person to die from a broken arm," he said softly.

Pippa glanced up quickly, her mouth parting in surprise. "I'm not worried about that. I only feel guilty."

"You needn't. You couldn't have known she was hurt."

Pippa scoffed. "Which is where you are wrong. I asked her if

56

she was hurt, and she responded that she was. I focused on getting her home. I hadn't thought that she *actually* hurt herself."

"Well, I was present for the exchange and thought nothing of it, either. If you are to blame, then I am in equal measure. Elinor even cradled her arm, so I should have noticed when I carried her."

"We are a sorry pair, are we not? We would make awful doctors."

"Speak for yourself." He tucked his chin. "I've attended Guy's Hospital and am quite adept at diagnosing most things."

Pippa's eyes bulged. "*You* are a doctor?"

"No, that was a joke," he said, grinning. He leaned forward and lowered his voice, catching that faint floral scent again as he lost himself in her dark blue-violet eyes. "But I find that I rather enjoy shocking you."

Pippa's smile was warm. She reached over and opened the front door. Light and cold air swept over them, and William was hesitant to leave. He slid his arms into his coat and tugged lightly on his cravat. "Until we meet again, Miss Sheffield."

She dipped in a light curtsy.

"Preferably sooner rather than later," he added, sending her an impertinent wink before stepping outside.

He thought he heard her sharp intake of breath, and triumph ran through his veins as he strode away.

CHAPTER 7

*P*ippa prepared the platter of tea and biscuits and carried it upstairs. It had been nearly a week since Elinor fell and broke her arm, nearly a week since Pippa had welcomed William into her house for tea, and she hadn't seen the man since. She hadn't left the house very much at all in that time, and she was nearly mad from the lack of direct sunlight on her skin.

She knocked softly before pushing Gram's door open, and she stepped inside the dimly lit room. Gram sat on a rocking chair near the fire, her brittle hands resting in her lap.

"Can I open the drapes, or do you prefer the room to be dark and depressing?" Pippa asked, raising her voice to be heard.

Gram's pinched lips didn't so much as twitch. "You want to give me grapes that you've pressed? Is that your modern term for wine, Pip?"

"No, no wine, Gram. Can I open the *drapes*?"

"I suppose I'll take some grapes. But I do not want wine. You know how it does not agree with me. Tea, please. Only tea."

Pippa suppressed a smile. "Very well, here is your tea." She put the platter down and poured a cup for Gram, handing it into her trembling fingers before moving the plate of biscuits closer.

Gram slurped noisily at her tea, and Pippa wondered if she was aware of how loudly she drank. She crossed the room, tugging open the drapes and looking back to gauge her grandmother's reaction, but she didn't appear displeased with the added light.

"Mabel let me read her last letter from Charles," Gram said, setting her tea cup down and taking a biscuit. "He is to have another baby soon."

"Yes, Gram, *quite* soon," Pippa agreed. Her cousin Charles's wife had been pregnant for nearly nine months now. The babe was set to arrive any day. Pippa poured herself a cup of tea and added a large chunk of sugar.

"Will they bring the children to visit soon, do you think?" Gram asked. Her mouth turned down at the ends. "I do enjoy having them here, though they are quite noisy."

Pippa took a sip of tea and coughed, covering her mouth with her wrist. Charles and Amelia's children were considered noisy? Did Gram not hear James and Elinor make their own ruckus daily? To say nothing for baby Liam.

"I'm certain Amelia will not be in a state to visit in quite some time, but she will come to us when she can." While the drive to Graton, where Pippa had been born and her sister lived most of her life, wasn't too far, it was far enough to warrant caution when one was about to give birth. "Has Elinor come to see you?"

"Yes," Gram said, taking a bite of her biscuit. "She will not find a husband while her arm is in that horrid contraption."

"She is five, Gram. She will heal well before that becomes a concern." Not that an arm brace would in any way come between Elinor and a husband, of course, had she been fifteen years older.

"She told me of the dashing hero that came to her aid,"

Gram said, a smile tugging at her lips as she reached for another biscuit. "A handsome man, was he?"

Handsome was attributed to men like Mac, or their good friend Hattie's husband, the duke. No, William Blakemore wasn't merely handsome. He was devastatingly attractive. Swallowing that traitorous thought, Pippa merely nodded.

"Well, who is he?" Gram pressed. "These old bones haven't been house-ridden for long, and I haven't seen a handsome face in Collacott in years."

"I'll tell Mac you said so."

"Hmm?" Gram asked, tilting her head in confusion.

Pippa raised her voice. "I will tell Mac you said so."

It took a moment, but Gram's lips flattened when she understood the joke. "Mac is not available, and you well know it. I'm thinking for *you*, Pip."

Need she remind everyone in her family that she was only nineteen years of age? Mabel had been six-and-twenty when she married Mac. The way Pippa saw it, she had another five years before she needed to hunt for a husband seriously. She had time on her side. She needn't pounce on every half-decent-looking man who crossed through their small coastal town. No matter how easily that man seemed to make her pulse race.

"I'm afraid Elinor's savior is quite off the table, as well."

"Why was he on the table?" Gram asked, leaning forward, her eyebrows bunching her wrinkled skin.

"No . . . I just mean . . ." Pippa gave up. "You will likely meet him, Gram. He's our nearest neighbor now."

"A near neighbor?"

Pippa understood her grandmother's confusion. No other house was within a reasonable distance, so out of the way they lived at Camden Court. "They've moved into Ravenwood Cottage."

Gram's body froze. When she spoke, her voice was low and

steady, sending a shiver down Pippa's spine. "Do not say Black Heart Blakemore has returned."

"Richard Blakemore has, yes, and he's brought his son William and their cousin Roger with him." Pippa laughed uncomfortably, the sound hollow. "Is that concerning?"

"Yes. When he lived here, the man's reputation reached Graton alongside his smuggled goods." Gram narrowed her eyes at her tea. "Do not mistake me, we were glad of the sugar and tea—your grandfather was glad of the brandy. Even your papa bought smuggled wine often. But Black Heart Blakemore had a reputation for ruthlessness that frightened me, even then."

Surely the pleasant-faced man who'd greeted Pippa's family politely in the churchyard last week could not be so ruthless. His weather-beaten skin had been the only element of roughness on his person. His tone, his smile, his clothing even, had all been exceptionally beyond reproach.

"I will be wary," Pippa said, hoping to appease her worried grandmother.

"Hmm?" Gram asked, leaning closer and turning her ear toward Pippa.

Pippa suppressed a smile. "I will be *wary*," she repeated loudly.

Gram shook her head. "Be more than wary, Pippa. Be vigilant."

It was difficult to shake the concern deeply coloring Gram's warning, or the resulting uneasiness which settled deep in Pippa's bones. Perhaps the Blakemore men truly did embody the wolf in Elinor's favorite story, shadowing themselves in a cloak of charisma and nice clothing. Gram's warning was branded onto Pippa's worries, and she was unable to shake it.

"Elinor's savior might be handsome, but I would stay far away from him," Gram said.

Pippa nodded, drinking her tea.

Gram settled back in her seat, adjusting her position. She

looked around the platter, scooting aside the small plate of biscuits, confusion clouding her expression. "Now, where are my grapes?"

When the sun fell through the long windows of the drawing room toward the end of the afternoon, the entire back wall lit orange and red, the wallpaper glowing and a hazy, warm incandescence settling upon the room. It was one of Pippa's favorite moments of the day. If she could not watch the sun make its final descent over the horizon from the beach, she enjoyed sitting in the drawing room and soaking in the toasty sunbeams.

"Pippa, it is your turn again," James said, mild frustration edging his words.

She looked to the chessboard sitting on the small table between them and slid the bishop over.

James huffed. "You are not even trying to win." He knocked over the bishop and removed it from the board.

He wasn't wrong, and Pippa's cheeks warmed slightly. She'd been so distracted since her conversation with Gram earlier that day and hadn't had half a mind to devote to the game. Pushing aside thoughts of the Blakemore men, she analyzed her pieces with greater attention. James must have been giving half an effort, for he could have won by now. She'd been moving her pieces directly into his path.

Sliding her knight around a pawn, Pippa sat back and waited for James to take his turn.

Mabel came into the room, Elinor close on her heels.

"Where is Liam?" Pippa asked.

Mabel pointed at the ceiling. "Napping. And I am going to take this time to catch up on my embroidery. I want to add a vine to that cap I made for Amelia's new little one." She sat, pulling her basket closer toward her on the floor. "Or do you think I should leave it be?"

"A green vine? Or whitework?"

"I had thought to do green. She has plenty of whitework."

"Then yes, I think you should."

Elinor huffed. "I do not want to embroider, Mama. I want to go outside."

"And injure yourself further?" Mabel clicked her tongue. "You may go outside to play when I am confident that you will mind your arm. You wish for it to heal properly, do you not?"

"No, I do not," Elinor said, scowling. "I care not for silly things like arms."

Pippa suppressed her amusement and looked down at the chessboard to avoid laughing at her niece. Elinor was serious in her stubbornness, and Pippa felt for her.

"You'll want use of both of your arms if you wish to easily climb a tree," James said.

Elinor seemed to consider this, and Mabel shot a look at Pippa. Pippa's hands went up in surrender. "I've taught her nothing."

Mabel narrowed her gaze. She shook her head and turned her attention to her embroidery.

"You shall need both of your arms if you intend to hold any kittens," Pippa said.

Elinor looked sharply at her. "That is true."

"What kittens?" Mabel asked.

Pippa only shrugged, and Elinor looked decidedly mischievous.

Mabel looked at her daughter a moment longer before shaking her head. "It has been nearly a week since we invited the Blakemores to dine. We really ought to schedule a dinner soon."

"You want to invite them here? Have you spoken with Gram about our new neighbors?" Pippa asked, looking from James to

Mabel. She seemed to garner the attention of them both, though Elinor continued to pout.

Mabel shook her head. "No, does she know them? She has only lived in this house as long as we have."

"Their reputation reaches far wider than Collacott's boundaries." Pippa wanted to say more, but not in the presence of the children. If Mabel wished for James and Elinor to be aware of the situation, that was her decision to make. She widened her eyes at James.

"You do realize that I am ten, not two," he said dryly. "I can see that you are pointing to me, and I wish to know these rumors as well."

"You'll not hear another word until I know how extensive the rumors are, James," Mabel said. "Run along, both of you, and let me speak to Pippa in privacy."

James groaned. "But we are not finished with our game."

"We can finish later. I will not touch a single piece," Pippa promised.

It took a few minutes more before both of the children left and the door closed behind them. Pippa crossed the room to sit beside her sister, pulling her ankles beneath her and admiring the beginning of the green vine against the white baby cap in her sister's hands.

"Well, get on with it," Mabel said, shooting her a smile.

Pippa relayed Gram's warnings from earlier about Black Heart Blakemore, how they had bought his smuggling goods, but had been wary of the man who supplied them.

"Even Papa bought smuggled wine. Did you know this?"

"Yes, but I didn't think much of it then." Mabel pulled her thread through the cap and offered Pippa an understanding smile.

"That is breaking the law."

"It is, but most people do not see it that way. Taxes have changed, but they used to be exorbitant. Purchasing smuggled goods was the only way we could get our hands on sugar, tea, or wine during the war."

Pippa shook her head. She'd been a child then and hadn't known. "But this reputation Gram heard about Mr. Blakemore seemed to worry her."

"A lot can change in twenty years, Pip," Mabel said softly. "I do think we ought to be cautious, but we should not cut them merely because of a rumor. Susan spent some time this week with the Blakemores while they placed orders for bedclothes and other linens, and she had nothing but good things to report. They were courteous and polite."

"So we ought to wait until they've harmed us or one of our friends before we know the extent of the danger they pose?"

"No, we ought to be cautious, as I said. Inviting them to dine will not lead to our demise." Mabel lowered her embroidery. "Why are you judging them so harshly? This is unlike you."

Why, indeed? Pippa couldn't explain it to herself even, except that William made her feel things that were uncomfortable and foreign, and she wanted nothing to do with those feelings. Which meant that she wanted nothing to do with *him*. But if that were truly the case, then why could she think of little else?

"Lily has been working for them for nearly a week, and I've not seen or spoken to her since Sunday. I suppose I am a little nervous for her sake."

"Mac saw Mr. Burke in town yesterday, and he reported that Lily is enjoying working for the Blakemores. I'm certain she'll tell you more at church tomorrow."

Pippa nodded. She needed to breathe, and it was far too difficult to inhale fully. She yearned for fresh sea air and a brisk wind to clear her head. "I think I will walk down to the cove before it gets too dark."

Mabel looked to the window, the orange glow warming her

pale skin. "It is nearly too dark already. Do not go down to the beach tonight, please."

"Very well, I won't go *down*." She grinned. "I'll stay on the high path."

Mabel looked as though she meant to argue, but she bit her tongue. Finding a comfortable rhythm between them now that Pippa was an adult was still taking time, but Mabel was making an effort to give Pippa the freedom to govern herself.

She rose, stretching her tired limbs. "I just want to see the sunset, Mabel."

"Do so quickly, then."

"Yes, I'll mention that to the sun. *Excuse me, could you please hurry it up? My sister doesn't wish to worry.*"

"At least you understand that my worry is for your sake and not merely to ruin your fun."

"Yes, and I love you for it." Pippa grinned at her sister before flouncing from the room. She retrieved her spencer jacket and buttoned it as she walked outside, not bothering with her bonnet. She hated the blasted things and how the wind pulled at them and ruined her hair.

The light was fading, the sun falling in a soft sky of faded blue to orange. Pippa walked the pathway, standing on the cliff-side and watching the sun dip lower and lower as she turned Gram's warning and Mabel's compassionate responses over in her mind. As it stood, William Blakemore confused and enticed her, and she was frightened of how that made her feel.

Pippa wrapped her arms around her middle and watched the sun descend as the water below her turned darker, the white caps bright against the navy water. Cold air swirled her skirts around her legs and danced loose hair across her forehead, and she breathed deeply.

Her neck prickled with awareness, and she turned, spotting a figure down in the cove walking along the sand. He stopped near the water, seemingly heedless of the wave lapping his feet.

Pippa squinted, looking closer. No, he wouldn't care if the water touched his feet, because his boots had been removed and left further up the beach. It would appear that William Blakemore liked to walk in the surf.

And Pippa was going to join him.

CHAPTER 8

*W*illiam let the cold water rush over his ankles, shocking his skin. He closed his eyes and breathed, pushing Roger and his obnoxious whining from his thoughts completely. The man was worse than a five-year-old. No, not worse. He was *as bad* as a five-year-old. And William would know. He'd carried a distraught child home from the beach just a week ago, and she'd whimpered and whined for the duration of the walk, much as Roger had been doing all week.

One would think that after years of smuggling it would be seamless to shift into the role of a fisherman. And while it had taken some practice the first few nights, William was growing proficient at fishing for the most part.

Well, that was untrue. He was awful at it. But he didn't despise it as much as Roger did. For William, it was hardly different from rowing out to collect smuggled goods, yet with the added benefit of not breaking the law.

Another wave rolled down the sand, dousing his ankles and running up his calves faster than he expected. William hadn't noticed that he'd walked further toward the water, and he backed up quickly before his thighs could be soaked.

A light, feminine laugh pricked his ears, and he turned sharply. His foot slipped on the waterlogged sand and sent him sprawling down into the surf. Water seeped through his side, chilling his skin immediately. He felt the wave recede and pushed up on his elbow in time to see Pippa standing in the distance, her eyes widened and fastened on him.

"William—" she called, her hand up as she started to run toward him.

He hardly had time to register that she had used his Christian name before he was alerted to another wave rushing toward him. The icy water hit his feet, and he sucked in a quick breath, pushing up from the ground before he could take a bath in the seawater. He wasn't averse to bathing in the sea, but he preferred not to be fully clothed and with an audience.

Pippa reached his side, panting and squeezing her waist. "I did not know if you saw the wave coming," she explained, breathless.

He nodded. Water dripped from his clothes and sand was pasted to his side. He really ought to go swim through the waves just to remove the beastly sand. But he could wait until she left.

"Were you laughing at me?" he asked.

Her cheeks rounded, and she looked to the water. "I couldn't help it. You looked as though you were practicing a Scottish reel in the waves."

William could see how he would have appeared that way, hopping backward as the wave approached. "Are you fond of dancing?" he asked.

Pippa brushed a loose strand of hair from her face, smiling. "Yes. Particularly lively reels."

"Oh? I would have taken you for a minuet kind of lady."

Her nose scrunched up. "Self-important and boring, you mean?"

She was the opposite of both of those descriptors, but he couldn't help it. He enjoyed trying to get a rise out of her. "Well, obviously."

Pippa narrowed her eyes, stepping closer. "Do you want to know what type of dance you appear to me?"

"Yes." He did want to know. Badly.

Her mouth ticked up in a wicked smile, one that drew his gaze like a ship to a lighthouse. "A waltz."

"Oh?" He had expected her to say a quadrille, or something sedate. To make a joke as he'd done. "Why is that?"

"You are scandalous, but everyone seems to love you anyway."

A laugh ripped from William's chest, rolling out into the twilight with abandon. He hadn't felt this light in some time, and while her words were true, they'd surprised him. The evening took on a hazy glow as the sun reached the edge of the world where the sea met the sky.

Holding Pippa's gaze, William's shoulders relaxed for the first time all day. "Why do you say that as though it is a troublesome thing to you?"

"Because I've been warned to be wary of your family's reputation, but the very same people who caution me don't seem too concerned after making your acquaintance. I cannot tell if it is magical trickery, if you are a wolf hiding in Little Red Riding Hood's grandmother's bed, or if you are truly as wonderful as you seem."

The truth and utter frankness of her words shocked him more than the sea's cold depths ever could. *Truly as wonderful as you seem.* So, she thought he seemed wonderful? That filled his belly with warmth, and it took a moment for him to regain his mental balance. "Well, one of the three is correct, but I shan't tell you which," he said, giving her his best smile.

"Why not?"

"You wouldn't believe me if I did, would you? If I was a wolf or embroiled in magic, I would certainly try to deceive you, and if I admitted that I was wonderful, you couldn't know whether or not to trust me." He shrugged. "So I won't bother."

She smiled. Looking past his shoulder, she watched the sun for a moment as it dipped behind the earth. Her voice was sad when she spoke. "I should go."

"I can walk you to the top of the rise," he suggested, moving to collect his boots. He'd worry about removing the sand another way. William was not about to miss an opportunity to spend a few more minutes with this woman.

He sat on a rock as the blue sky turned darker. He'd spent too long out here and would need to get home soon before he lost the ability to see the way.

Pippa followed him to the rocks, waiting while he pulled his stockings on. She didn't avert her eyes, as he'd expected her to, and it only made him chuckle softly.

"How is Lily—er, Miss Burke, I suppose—doing in your kitchen?" she asked.

"For such a small space and not much to work with, she's been wonderful," he said.

Pippa nodded. "And she is being treated well?"

William shoved his feet into his boots before he stood and wiped his hands down his sandy, wet trousers. "Have you been concerned for her?"

"Yes," she said without delay. "Of course I would be worried. My friend has gone to cook for complete strangers."

"We are not strangers to all who live here," he reminded her. They began climbing the steep, rocky path up to the top of the rise.

"Yes, but those who knew you before did not originally sing your praises."

William halted on the path, reaching for Pippa's hand. He was surprised to find it unadorned, and he was grateful he'd stuffed his own gloves in his pocket earlier when he'd arrived down at the cove. Her skin was delightfully smooth, but he could feel the worn, rough patches here and there where she'd developed calluses. As he'd expected, Pippa was a little of both: rough and smooth. And he loved it.

"Why do you hold such prejudice against me, Pippa? I've known you but a week, and yet I feel I ought to work to prove myself."

"Because you are the sort of man who flirts without censure and uses Christian names willy nilly."

She didn't tug her hand free of his grip, and William rejoiced in the warm connection. She turned to face him better, and he stepped closer, their joint hands hanging between them. "I believe I was not the first to use a Christian name this evening without express permission."

Her eyes widened, glowing in the bleary twilight. "If I slipped, I assure you it wasn't intentional."

"Do not say that. You'll only disappoint me."

Pippa's lips flattened. "You cannot expect me to take you seriously when you speak such ridiculous things."

"Who is saying they are ridiculous? It wounds me that you would believe me to be inauthentic."

Pippa laughed. "See? Precisely that. You are a flirt, William, and I should hope you wouldn't speak to Lily in such a way. Not unless you are genuine."

He stilled. Pippa's fingers danced slightly, trying to break away, but he didn't want to lose the contact. Not yet. He ran his thumb over her palm, tracing the curved line that creased around her thumb. She froze beneath his touch; he was glad he had *something* of an effect on this perplexing creature.

Her warning was worrisome. He'd noticed Lily watching him, and he'd tried to be polite to the girl, but she hadn't captured his interest. Not like Pippa had.

"Perhaps you only tell yourself I'm not genuine because you don't wish for me to be."

Pippa shook her head. "There. Again with the ridiculousness. You couldn't be genuine, for I've known you a week, sir. One week."

"People have fallen in love in less time than that."

"Yes, but those people were not you and I."

William wanted her to be wrong. He liked this woman excessively. Her blunt manner, her ability to climb trees in a dress, her lack of bonnet leading to tanned cheeks and a dash of freckles over her nose—she was simply lovely. Perhaps he had not fallen in love with her in the space of a week, but he *had* grown genuinely interested in her.

"Do you have any suitors?" he asked, leaning forward and lowering his voice.

"No. Not a single one."

"Then I have time on my side." He released her hand, certain he'd left behind sand on her skin. He was thoroughly covered in it.

Pippa shook her head, but she didn't move. "You will regret those words, William. I have a penchant for getting into trouble."

"Then it is a good thing I've been called trouble once or twice in my life."

"Only once or twice?"

He grinned, and she turned around, climbing the steep path the rest of the way up to the top without the least concern. William had all but announced his interest in this woman and she'd brushed him off like he was a bothersome wasp. She paused at the top, looking over the dark sea and sunless sky.

"I suppose I will see you in church tomorrow?" she asked, her gaze sliding to meet his.

"You shall."

She smiled. "I'm glad to hear it. Goodnight, Mr. Blakemore."

"Goodnight, Pippa."

She turned to walk away from him, and he watched her until she reached the edge of the tree-lined drive that led to her house. When she was safely on her own property again, William turned toward home.

His feet squelched with every step as water slid down his legs and filled his boots. By the time he reached his cottage, it was dark and he followed the light from the windows to see. Lily would be long gone by now, thankfully. After Pippa's warning, William wasn't sure he wanted to see her so soon. Her little smiles and watchful gazes held much more meaning now.

William let himself into the cottage. He closed the door and kicked off his boots, inhaling the yeasty smell of baked bread.

"Where have you been?" Father asked, sitting on a chair near the fire. The room was sparse of furniture. William needed to order more if they planned to be at the cottage much longer. At present, they only had a handful of mismatched chairs and a dusty settee they'd found in the attic with an array of holes in it. There'd been beds enough, but flimsy, old mice-bitten mattresses, and after the feather clouds William was used to sleeping on, these hurt his back.

He lowered himself onto a rickety wooden chair and bent to peel off his sodden stockings.

"Walked down to the beach," William said. He wouldn't mention which one, for he didn't want anything to ruin the peace he'd felt on that stretch of sand. He'd liked seeing Pippa there tonight. In all of his solo walks in the last week, this was the first time he'd happened upon her. He'd hoped to see her before now but had been disappointed until this evening.

He'd chosen that particular beach for a reason.

"Have you found a good place for Jack to make the drop?"

"Do you not already have the location sorted?" William asked, shocked that his father had left *any* details until just weeks before they were meant to meet his brother.

"We'll shine the lantern from the peak at Camden Cove," Father said. "But the hole you dug won't be large enough for the loot. We need another place."

"What of the location you used when you lived here before?"

"Donewell Tunnel? It's caved in. John Caney told me so himself after church last week. You were there."

William recalled the man's joke, but he hadn't realized it was a message. "Is that not the prime location then? No one will think to look there if the place is caved in. Will they not dismiss it as readily as you've done?"

Father leaned back in his chair, seeming to consider this. He rubbed his stubbled chin and blew a long breath through his nose. "I see your point, but it's no use. If it's caved in, I assume there's no way to get inside."

Roger came down the stairs and lounged on the settee, his leg flung over the armrest. "Where've you been?"

"Walking again," Father mumbled. He looked at William. "Keep up your walks. No one will be wary of them, for you've already been doing it. Though heaven knows why," he muttered. "And keep an eye out for a sea cave or something we can use."

"Wouldn't you know of every cave or cavern in the area?" Roger asked, skeptical, it seemed, of William's ability to find a good hiding place. "Did you not live here for half your life? More, even?"

"Earth can move and shift," Father said. "The tunnel caved, and other places could have done the same. New caves could have formed. I would go out and look myself, but I don't have the mobility I once did."

"Which is why we need more men before we can meet Jack," William said. His brother had an entire crew on that ship and enough contraband to fill this cottage, more likely than not. He was a good businessman, which was why Father had appointed Jack as their French liaison. But even if Jack's men helped them unload the ship, they needed more men in Collacott to move the barrels. "Roger and I cannot do it all ourselves."

"I'll get us more men," Father said confidently. "We'll be going to church again tomorrow."

"Count me out." Roger leaned back and closed his eyes. "I've never been one for sermons or hymns. Too stodgy."

Mr. Robinson was the least stodgy clergyman William had ever before seen. If he was too boring for Roger, then the man's aptitude for paying attention was nonexistent.

William waited quietly. He thought for a moment that Father would argue, that he would force Roger to submit. They'd brought the man along to protect him, after all. The least he could do was to play his role.

Or perhaps that *was* what he was doing, playing the role of the bored fop who couldn't be bothered with religion—a fop who wore unembellished wool and lived in a cottage.

"Good, then you can remain behind and finish the mortar," Father said.

Roger's lips pressed flat, but he didn't argue. "Can we not hire more servants?"

"No." Father said no more, and the matter was dropped.

William chose to believe that his father had a plan that would restore him to his home in Dorset. This cottage suited William well enough, but it was incongruous with Richard Blakemore. The man had built a successful smuggling business out of Dorset that had supplied them with the income to live a life of relative ease. If evading revenue men and breaking the law could foster a sense of ease, that was.

Until he knew any differently, William would continue on as though this was their permanent home—and perhaps that could become the case for him. He wasn't cut out for smuggling, and it wasn't what he wanted to do for the remainder of his life. "We need to plant soon. We should prepare the south field by the end of next week."

"We won't be around when it's time to reap the benefits," Roger said, his blond eyebrows bunching. "Surely we needn't go so far in our ruse."

William leaned over to hang his stockings near the fire to dry before slouching from his coat. Once dry, it would be easy to beat the sand free of his clothes.

"It is not a ruse," Father said.

William froze. He tried to cover his surprise by arranging his coat on the back of his chair and moving it closer to the fire, but Father watched him closely, and he was certain the man noticed.

"Yes, and I am truly going to be a fisherman for the rest of my days," Roger said, laughter punctuating his words.

"You won't, no," Father said. He looked at William, the rest of his thought floating unspoken between them.

Roger won't, but William very well might.

All these years since Mother's death, and William had thought he'd done an excellent job of hiding his true feelings from his father. Evidently, he hadn't been as surreptitious as he'd thought. Either Father knew of William's acute dislike for the smuggling trade, or he believed William to truly enjoy this damp little cottage life.

Rising, William stretched his arm high above his head. "I need to get into dry clothes before we prepare to leave."

Roger groaned. "Must we fish *every* night?"

"Yes." William suppressed a chuckle. "Well, every night except Sunday."

"The one good thing about Sunday," Roger murmured. "I still do not quite understand why we cannot fish in the daylight."

"Easier to catch them when they don't see the nets coming," William said as he mounted the stairs. He heard Father mumble something to Roger but pushed them from his mind. He was, oddly enough, looking forward to getting out on the boat in the open sea again. He enjoyed the feeling of rowing the oars until he was so tired that he collapsed in his bed and fell asleep swiftly, despite the uncomfortable mattress.

He was growing content in this new way of life, but he had a feeling that it was false, that it couldn't last long.

And whatever it was that was coming to disrupt it, his father was surely behind it.

CHAPTER 9

*W*illiam slicked the sweat from his brow with the side of his wrist. He'd soaked his handkerchief in water and laid it over the back of his neck, but it wasn't doing much to cool him. Was a man meant to sweat this much when the weather was so mild? It bordered on cool, regardless of the sun beating high overhead. The breeze chilled his hot neck, and he scoffed at himself. He hadn't lived a sedentary life, but clearing and tilling the earth was backbreaking work.

He looked out over the field, frustrated by the minuscule size of the small plot of land he'd cleared and tilled. He'd spent the entirety of the morning working and *this* was all he had to show for it? William fought the frustration and exhaustion that tempted him to quit. Roger was sleeping and Father was no use, so why was he working so hard?

Well, if William didn't do the work, who would?

He scrubbed a hand over his face, hoping it would wake him more. They'd been out on the ocean late last night with mediocre success. It would take some time for William to grow adept at fishing, but he was enjoying the process thus far. He was grateful he'd saved enough money to feel as though he wasn't in a hurry to turn a profit quite yet.

Father's success at smuggling had allowed William to work hard and save bit by bit over the years. He had a tidy sum put away, and he fully intended to use part of it to furnish the cottage once things settled down a little more. He couldn't leave Jack without any help—they were brothers after all, and one did not leave one's brother in the lurch—but this was the final time.

William wanted to make a name for himself in Collacott, and he wanted it to be respectable. He found himself enjoying the area and the people. The men who fished together had something of a brotherhood, and they'd been welcoming—the opposite of what William had expected when he'd learned they were coming to a new town and joining the majority of the men in fishing the local water.

After watching his father speak to some of the congregation after church their first Sunday, William had questioned why they'd ever left Devonshire in the first place. Though he didn't truly have to look far to find the answer: his father enjoyed the finer things in life. The opulent home and feather mattresses they'd left behind in Dorset were just a few of the reasons they'd not lived in Devon for the last twenty years.

That, and Dorset was a much more sensical location for building a smuggling enterprise from France.

William returned to the place he'd left off and continued cutting away the weeds in order to till the earth. His arms grew tired and his back sore. Birds arched overhead, and he wished just a few of the thin white clouds would cross over the sun and give him a moment's reprieve.

Men's voices carried through the trees behind him, and William breathed a sigh of relief. He would gladly put up with Roger's complaints if it meant slicing his workload in half.

A tall figure broke through the treeline, and William stilled, surprised to find Mac walking his way. The man's tall frame blocked another gentleman behind him that William didn't recognize, and young James followed shortly.

"You must have gotten an early start," Mac called pleasantly.

William gripped his scythe and approached the men. He'd shed his coat and waistcoat earlier, opting to work in his shirt-sleeves and breeches. "What can I do for you?"

"We've come to help." Mac smiled pleasantly. "I told you the men of Collacott could be relied upon to be neighborly, did I not?"

If the men of Collacott consisted of these two gentlemen, then yes, William supposed that was true. He was not one to turn down help, and with their assistance, the speed at which this field was prepared could triple.

Grinning, William nodded. "Thank you, sir. It's much appreciated. I am grateful for both of your help." He winked at James. "And yours as well."

"It isn't just us," Mac said, looking back over his shoulder. No one appeared behind him, and William wondered if Mac was looking for Roger or William's father. If his statement had been, in fact, a question.

He began to excuse their absence, though he didn't know why he felt the need to protect either of them from censure. "My father's leg prevents him from assisting me, and Roger has other things to do—"

Mac sent him a curious look that made the rest of William's explanation die swiftly on his tongue. The man didn't appear to care for Roger's excuses.

Voices reached them, filtering through the trees as more men appeared. One by one they stepped out of the thin path in the foliage, filling in the empty space behind Mac until there was an army of workers standing at the ready. The men's willingness to help him made William's chest thick with gratitude, and he cleared his throat to cover the emotion welling within him.

"Where is Renwick?" Mac asked.

Another man with a large, bulbous nose flicked his head toward the pathway they'd just come through. "Couldn't make it through the wood, so he's going the long way 'round."

Mac nodded as though this made perfect sense to him, but William was lost. Who was Renwick, and why could the man not fit through the wood?

"We ought to wait for Renwick," Mac said. "But show us what you need done in the meantime."

William came to himself quickly, shaking his awe for the men around him. He couldn't believe how many had shown up to help. It was certainly a greater number than those who filled the pews on Sundays.

Mac watched him expectantly, and William nodded, filtering through his plans. He pointed to the small plot he'd already worked himself. "This is as far as I've gotten. I'd like to work this entire field."

"What of the field to the east?" the man with the bulbous nose asked, coming to stand beside Mac, his forehead lined in consideration.

"Eventually, yes." William looked to the larger field in the distance. "Someday."

A neigh stole his attention, and he glanced over his shoulder to find a man leading a slow, thickly built horse which dragged a cart holding an inverted plow. William's heart sped like a drum building its rhythm. Never in his life had he experienced such consideration, and it was doing odd things to his chest. That plow was going to cut down the time it would take to till his fields by an enormous margin. He was flummoxed.

Mac chuckled, slapping William on the back. He rocked forward, not expecting the force of Mac's gesture, and caught himself before he could fall. Mac directed the men where to go and told them what needed doing. He glanced back at William for approval, it seemed, but William just nodded. Everything Mac asked the men to do were all things on William's list. The man knew exactly what needed to be done to prepare these fields for a spring harvest.

"Welcome to Collacott," Mac said, before turning to help the man called Renwick with the plow.

This was a brilliant welcome, indeed.

CHAPTER 10

*P*ippa removed the pear tarts from the cooling rack and stacked them in the basket resting on the counter. Afternoon light streamed through the narrow kitchen windows and highlighted the pale cream linen hanging over the side of the wicker basket. She filled it to the top and tucked the linen over the tarts, humming to herself.

"Shall we walk down or hook up the cart?" Mabel asked, filling the second basket with bread rolls. She handed a roll to Elinor, who took a large bite directly from the top, and then covered the rolls with linen.

"When are we meant to arrive?"

Mabel shook her head, looking flustered. "A quarter-hour ago, but we're only going to the Blakemores' cottage. I'm certain dinner will have already begun, regardless of how we travel."

"Where is James?"

"I sent him ahead with Mac and Winthrop. You know, I think we should take the cart in case Liam doesn't wish to stay very long. His teeth are coming in and he's been fussing more." Mabel hooked the basket over her elbow. "Elinor, run and tell Hope that we are ready to leave."

Elinor huffed. She took another large bite of her roll and marched out of the kitchen. Her arm was wrapped and hanging at her side. Mabel gazed at the ceiling, her eyebrows drawn in thought.

Pippa pilfered a pear tart and sank her teeth into it. The syrupy sweetness exploded on her tongue, and the flaky pastry made her mouth water. Swallowing her bite, she followed her sister's gaze up to the space where she stared. It was the corner of the house that contained Grams's room. "Does it hurt you to leave Gram behind, too?"

Mabel nodded, folding her arms and resting her hip against the counter. Her eyes were troubled. "Yes, but she cannot travel easily. It is not as though we wish for her to remain home."

"I know that," Pippa said gently. "I am certain Gram understands as well."

Mabel blew out a long, slow breath that seemed to bend her shoulders forward. "I'm sure you're right."

Hope and Elinor met them outside, Liam sleepily bundled against his mother as Hope carried the bread basket and Pippa carried the tarts. Their cook and the handful of other servants who lived and worked at Camden Court were already at the Blakemore fields or the cottage, lending their help where they were able. Mabel always made certain someone was left behind to tend to Gram, but aside from that, the Sheffield household had gone in full force to support the Blakemores.

It was a far cry from the initial hesitance her family had shown the men, and Pippa found herself wondering if she was the only person left who recalled the awful reputation the Blakemores had carried into Devon with them.

Music and laughter warned them of the location of the feast long before they arrived in the proper place, and Pippa's chest loosened as she climbed down from the back of the cart and saw her familiar friends and family gathered together. Mac stood out, a head taller than most of the men gathered, and his eyes lit up when they landed on Mabel holding Liam.

"Come," Mabel said, directing Elinor. She hadn't seemed to notice the effect her arrival had had on her husband, her focus solely on the children. "Take those rolls from Hope so we can put them on the table."

Elinor did as she was asked, and Hope took Liam from Mabel's arms as he began to fuss, bouncing him and swaying from side to side. Pippa searched the crowds for William but didn't find him on her initial glance. She made her way slowly through the crowd, surprised by the sheer number of people who had shown up to help.

Someone yanked on her arm, and she almost lost her hold on the basket of tarts.

"Oh, sorry!" Lily said, though her wide smile belied any claimed apology. "I called your name, but you didn't seem to hear me."

Pippa hadn't heard anything of the sort. She'd been too distracted in her search for William, it would seem.

But could she be blamed for wanting to see him again? A man did not touch her hand so gently and then leave her mind forthwith. She'd hardly been able to think of anything else since that tender moment on the beach, and she wanted nothing more than to recreate it. Perhaps she could lose her gloves tonight on the guise of . . . no, nothing came to mind. She could think of no legitimate reason to remove her gloves in the cold, outside, in the evening.

"I was distracted," she finally said.

"So it would seem." Lily pulled her to the side, away from people, her eyes bright with excitement. "Why are you so distracted, Pip?"

Pippa could hardly admit the truth. It wouldn't make her look good to say that she was thinking of a man who had sweetly caressed her palm three days before. "Tell me about yourself instead," Pippa said. "I feel like I haven't spoken to you in ages."

Lily's eyes were bright and wide, her grin untamable. She radiated joy in a way that Pippa hadn't seen from her friend in quite some time. Since before Tommy grew ill, in fact. "Is it your brother?" she asked. "Is he well?"

"He is here today," Lily said, but some of the enthusiasm had drained from her voice. "He's feeling much more the thing."

"James will be glad to see him."

"They've been together this last hour already."

An hour? Pippa had arrived later to the feast than she'd realized. She suppressed the urge to look about her for William again and focused her attention on her friend, drawing the basket handle back to the crook of her elbow. "If your brother's health isn't owed to your good mood, then what is?"

Lily stepped closer, her eyes sparkling. "If I tell you, then you must promise not to repeat a word of what I say."

"Only if your safety is not in jeopardy."

"Promise, Pippa."

"I do promise," she said. "As long as your safety is not in question. I will not alter that."

"My safety?" Lily laughed. "You are too much."

"You cook for Black Heart Blakemore, so you must understand my desire to be cautious."

Lily's golden eyebrows drew together, and she tilted her head softly to the side. "You need to trust people, Pip."

Pippa scoffed. "They need to earn it, first. I trust plenty in those who deserve it."

Lily looked as though she meant to argue but changed her mind. A smile curved her lips into a wide arch, and she lowered her voice. "I believe Mr. Blakemore may hold me in high regard."

A rock fell into the pit of Pippa's stomach, and she did her best to cover her surprise.

Lily didn't seem to notice. "I never thought it could be possible, that I could be the object of such a man's affection."

Pippa raised her finger, pointing it directly at her friend's chest. "You are worth—"

"Yes, I know how you feel," Lily said impatiently, pushing Pippa's hand back down. "But the world does not see things the way you do."

That was the truth of it. Pippa had been fortunate to grow up in a household that valued people for who they were. Her family had servants, but they cared about them. Hope had been Pippa's nursery maid when she was a young girl, and when given the choice, had opted to move to Camden Court with them. She still resided in their house, working for them and helping to care for Mabel's children, but she was valued and loved.

Most of England would find Hope's relationship to their family odd, but Pippa didn't care.

"That is hardly relevant now," Lily said, lowering her voice and leaning closer. "Mr. Blakemore is the kindest, most handsome man I've ever beheld, and I think he might feel something for me."

The rock grew heavier in Pippa's stomach. "What has led you to think this?"

"Because of the way he speaks to me," Lily whispered. "The way he looks at me and how his voice grows soft and kind. I wouldn't have considered his affection to be real, but you planted that seed of potential in my heart, and now I cannot help but hope, and I think it is a glorious thing."

"What sort of potential?"

Lily's cheeks pinked, and she dipped her head. "I found myself wondering if someone like you could befriend me so wholly, could a man not do the same? Perhaps even love me?"

"You've known this man for a week." Panic gripped Pippa's chest and tightened. She hadn't meant to set her friend up for false expectations. She wanted Lily to understand her own worth, but she wasn't clueless. Pippa realized that most men wouldn't see things the way she did.

"Eleven days," Lily corrected airily. "But it feels more like a lifetime."

Pippa took great care not to look too disbelieving. Fault lay like a heavy bag of bricks on her shoulders. It was because of her that Lily entertained these notions at all. "None of these things are exactly sturdy signs of his affection, though."

"Well, they might not be, but I will not let that dissuade me yet." Lily grinned, shaking her head. "I do not believe a proposal is imminent, Pip, but I do think something is blooming between Mr. Blakemore and myself."

Pippa drew in a breath, squared her shoulders, and took her friend's hand. Lily wasn't being unreasonable. She was merely excited for a potential romance. Glancing at the crowd, Pippa found William standing between his cousin and Mac. He glanced up and looked directly at her as if he'd known where she was before she located him. He must have recently arrived there, for he hadn't been speaking to Mac when Pippa's wagon pulled up.

William nodded along to whatever it was Mac was saying, but his gaze was settled on Pippa. Her chest heated, her core clenching with awareness and Lily's confession ringing freshly in her ears. He could not truly feel anything for Lily if he was going to look at Pippa in such a way, could he? Or perhaps he wasn't looking at Pippa at all. The possibility that he could be lovingly gazing at *Lily* and Pippa only misinterpreted it brought reality over her like a swift bucket of seawater.

"Pippa, are you listening?"

Pippa turned toward Lily abruptly, and the basket of tarts flew off her arm, tumbling down to the straw-strewn ground. "Drat!"

"Oh, no!"

Pippa knelt and turned the basket over. Luckily she had

tucked the linen tightly enough that most of the pastries had been saved. But there were two casualties, sitting in the dirt and covered in brown specks.

She rose and brushed the knees of her deep blue gown. "Most of them are safe. I better get these to the table."

Lily lifted the linen and took a tart. "I should check on Mama. She wasn't feeling well, but Papa convinced her to come anyway."

"Did she catch your brother's cold?"

"No, nothing like that. Exhaustion, I believe. She's taken on far more laundry than she should have these last few weeks, if you ask me." Lily took a bite of the tart and groaned in delight.

Pippa squeezed her friend's hand before turning to make her way toward the tables.

Pippa glanced toward Mac and found him speaking to Roger, William missing from their circle. She faced the table. Plates and baskets covered the space with more food than they could possibly consume as a whole. Pies, hams, rolls, and sliced apples and pears overflowed the tables. People milled about, eating from plates and chatting amiably.

William stepped up beside her, and Pippa's entire body reacted with alertness to his presence. She wasn't entirely sure what it was that he did to her heart, but she knew it beat a double rhythm, its pace increasing with his proximity. It would be best to fight her growing attraction to this man, but she didn't want to.

Pippa didn't entirely trust William, but she hoped she eventually could. And there was only one way to do so . . . she needed to get to know him better.

CHAPTER 11

*P*ippa clutched the basket of pear tarts close to her side and did her best not to look too eager to be in William's presence. Could he tell how immensely difficult it was for her to stand still and appear unaffected?

"Did you suffer many losses when your basket fell?" he asked, clasping his hands behind his back and standing on wide, steady legs. He clearly did not struggle with the same difficulty to remain calm and unaffected in her presence that she did in his, for he looked quite naturally at ease.

It made her want to ruffle his composure.

Pippa wedged her basket into the open space she'd created on the table and took a tart. "Only two. But they will make a good treat for the birds tomorrow."

"You and those birds," William said, mocking utter awe. "It is incredible how you look out for their well-being."

"Someone needs to," Pippa said.

"Do they, though?"

She grinned, unable to dampen her amusement. "Of course they do, and I am the perfect person for the position."

"I would have to agree on that final score, at least."

Pippa chuckled, sinking her teeth into a delicious pear tart. She'd lost track of how many she'd eaten thus far. Perhaps she ought to be in charge of the rolls next time, for they were far less easy to overindulge in.

William seemed to be moving closer, though Pippa couldn't tell if it was a trick of her eye or reality. He wore only his shirt-sleeves and a waistcoat, and she forced her gaze not to linger anywhere other than his face. *Drat*. That was far too easy to get lost in, as well.

"Tell me," he said, his voice too low and throaty for a conversation tucked in the middle of such a large gathering. "What do you—"

"You tell me," she countered, afraid of what he'd been about to ask. "How is Lily?"

She'd caught him by surprise. His eyes widened, his thick, dark eyebrows crawling together. "She is a better cook than the woman we hired in Dorset."

Pippa hadn't asked about Lily's cooking. She'd asked about Lily and hoped to learn whether or not William felt anything for her. Evidently, William was going to make this harder than she'd hoped. "Yes, I imagine she is. Lily is a talented cook." Pippa popped the remainder of her pear tart in her mouth and chewed, discerning the best way to phrase this information-gathering question.

"That looks delicious," William said, staring at her lips.

She immediately quit chewing, the tart congealing and drying her mouth. With great effort, Pippa swallowed the remainder of her tart and looked about for something to drink. William had other ideas. He stepped closer and lifted his thumb to brush something from her bottom lip.

Pippa froze. Her skin sizzled where he'd touched her and her breath caught, then suspended completely. She wanted to step back, but she was afraid the motion would draw attention to them. Was William completely reckless, or merely a fool?

"The entire town is here," she said, rubbing her gloved fingers over her lip where he'd seared her. His gloves were decidedly absent, which she found unfair.

"I noticed."

Ah, so he was completely reckless then. Pippa looked about for Lily to see if she'd noticed William's gesture, but she was nowhere near. In fact, it didn't appear that anyone was paying them any mind. Lucky, that.

William continued, unperturbed. "I owe your brother-in-law an enormous debt. If Mac hadn't organized the men of Collacott to clear and plow my fields, I would still be clearing them come April."

He'd missed the point completely. He wasn't reckless then, merely a fool. "It would be difficult to harvest if you haven't planted anything."

"Indeed, I wouldn't have been able to without all this help." Dipping his head slightly, he held her gaze. "I need your help to discern a suitable way to thank Mac."

"You might start by not ruining his sister-in-law's reputation."

"I hardly think clearing crumbs from your chin will *ruin* you, Pippa."

She swallowed both a gasp and the temptation to swat his arm. So he *did* know what he'd been doing when he'd slid a finger over her lip. *The cad.* Chin? He hadn't even brushed her chin.

She tapped a finger thoughtfully against her lips. "You wiped away crumbs that I did not even feel, Mr. Blakemore. Hmmm. Curious, that. How do I know they were truly there at all? How can I be certain you were not merely looking for an excuse to . . ."

"Yes?" he asked, tilting his head to the side in feigned confusion. The sparkle in his eye belied his pretended bewilderment about what she could possibly have meant to say.

Pippa's cheeks warmed. "You know perfectly well what I implied."

"Not truly, no," he said. "You could have meant to ask if I was looking for an excuse to distract you in order to steal a tart."

"You needn't steal a tart, though, for they are meant for everyone." Pippa lifted an arm and swept it over the table. "In fact, this entire feast was designed for your benefit."

"Was it, now? I thought it was an excuse for the people of Collacott to come together and feast."

"True," Pippa conceded. "Perhaps that was the goal all along, and your fields were merely the avenue to help us reach this point."

"It wouldn't bother me if that were the case. I still have the benefit of two perfectly plantable fields."

"They haven't been planted yet?" Pippa asked, reaching for another pear tart. At this rate, she was going to have a queasy stomach before the night was over. She ought to balance these tarts with a meat pie or a roll. Where did Mabel's rolls go?

William chuckled. "No, but I need to obtain the seeds. I hadn't expected to have such a large field to plant. You would be shocked to see the small plot I had cleared and tilled myself."

"I'm certain I would have been impressed by what you managed to accomplish. I can hardly weed our small garden myself."

William crossed his arms over his chest and looked at her with interest. "You weed your own gardens? Is this something you do for pleasure?"

"Yes, though it didn't start out that way. My sister used it as a punishment when I was young—"

"Pip, can you take Liam?" Mabel asked, approaching with the babe and all but thrusting him into Pippa's unsuspecting arms. The gesture caused her to drop the last bite of her tart on the ground. "There's a situation with Elinor and I can't find Mac."

"Of course." Pippa propped Liam on her hip, and he whined, reaching for his mother as she lifted her hem and hurried away.

Where was Hope? And Mac? Pippa looked around but didn't see either of them in the crowd. She must have been the convenient choice. She looked up at William.

"A situation?" he asked.

"That did not sound good."

"No, it did not. Perhaps we ought to confirm that everyone is well."

She nodded, falling into step beside William as they weaved their way through the gathered groups of people in the direction Mabel had gone. No screaming or sounds of distraught girls met her ears, so Pippa had to assume Elinor was neither hurt nor in immediate danger. They rounded the house and came to an abrupt halt. Elinor sat on a branch in a beech tree, her arms around the trunk while tears streamed down her face.

"Come to me, darling. I promise not to let you fall." Mabel spoke softly, her arms raised to her daughter.

Elinor shook her head. "I cannot let go."

"You must let go if you do not wish to spend your night in that tree. Now, please come down."

William brushed past Pippa, coming to stand beside Mabel. He rested his hands on his hips and looked up at Elinor. The branch she sat upon was not much taller than him. Surely he could reach her if he stretched.

"Goodness, Miss Mackenzie," William said. "I would almost wonder if you keep getting yourself into scrapes merely so I might rescue you."

Elinor froze, looking down at William with confused interest. Her red, splotchy cheeks shone with tears in the waning sunlight.

William lifted an eyebrow. "I do enjoy playing the hero, Miss Mackenzie, but there are much better ways of gathering my attention than getting yourself caught in a tree."

Elinor giggled. She wiped her runny nose with the back of her bandaged arm and Mabel sucked in a breath. How long had she been trying to convince Elinor to let go of the tree before choosing to relieve herself of Liam?

"I don't wish to step on any toes," William said. "But would it be acceptable if I carried you down, Miss Mackenzie?"

Elinor's eyes widened, and she glanced from William to her mother. She shook her head, fear gleaming in her worried countenance.

"You needn't jump to me," he soothed. "I will reach up and hold your waist, and you do not need to let go of the tree until you feel safe. Is that agreeable to you, Miss Mackenzie?"

Elinor looked at her mother again, and Mabel gave a brief nod of encouragement.

Elinor nodded hesitantly.

"Perhaps once you are safely down, you can show me what delightful pastry your mother has supplied for the party?" William asked.

"Oh, those are pear tarts."

William made a face, scrunching his nose in disgust. "*Pear* tarts? Oh, how awful. Do not tell me you like pear tarts?"

Elinor laughed. "I love them. You would too if you tried them."

"I think not," William said. "I despise pears and all things relating to them."

"These are different. They aren't like normal pears. They're in *tarts*."

William made a show of considering this. "You propose the idea that I might enjoy them just because they are wrapped in pastry and cinnamon? Hmmm. That is an interesting concept. If I help you down, then perhaps we can try them together." He reached toward her, and she hesitated only slightly before placing her good hand on his shoulder and holding her injured arm against her chest.

William took her by the waist and lifted her from the branch, setting her softly on the ground.

Mabel released a long, relieved breath and took Liam from Pippa's arms. Speaking quietly, she leaned close. "Good heavens, that had me worried. Elinor was too nervous to jump to me. She feared hurting her arm again."

"Thank heavens for Mr. Blakemore," Pippa said.

"Truly," Mabel agreed. She evidently hadn't picked up on the dryness of Pippa's words. Mabel raised her voice to be heard by William. "We will soon be in trouble if you continue to rescue my children, Mr. Blakemore. I need to find a way to repay your kindness."

A smile spread over William's lips. "I think I could rescue them a dozen times over and still be in your debt. You cannot know how grateful I am for what your husband did for me today."

Mabel nodded, adoration gleaming in her eyes. "He is a thoughtful man. I do hope you feel welcomed to Collacott, Mr. Blakemore. We must schedule a time to have you and your family over for dinner. Perhaps after church on Sunday?"

"I think that would be wonderful." William looked at Pippa, his eyes full of meaning, and she had difficulty breaking her gaze away. He had come to Elinor's rescue twice now with no enticement. He'd merely acted out of the goodness of his heart. Perhaps he was more trustworthy than Pippa had allowed herself to believe.

Liam fussed again, his tiny wail piercing the joyous conversation. Someone on the far end of the clearing had brought out a violin and the lilting string music drifted over the people.

"It sounds as though there will be dancing?" William said, though he voiced it as a question.

Mabel nodded, bouncing her unhappy babe. "You now know where our priorities lie, Mr. Blakemore. Here in Collacott, music and dancing rule the day. I think our people will use just about any excuse to come together to eat and dance."

William nodded sagely. "Eating and dancing. What more do we need in life?"

Pippa removed one of her gloves and handed it to Liam, who put it in his mouth greedily, chewing on the fawn leather. It quieted him, but she knew it wouldn't do so for long.

"If you are truly of that opinion, sir, you fit in quite well already." Mabel looked over her shoulder before offering them an apologetic smile. "I must go find my husband. I think Liam would like to go home soon. Pip, will you keep an eye on Elinor?"

"Of course."

Mabel slipped away, and Elinor huffed. "I do not need looking after. No one is looking after James."

"I don't believe James found himself stuck in a tree this evening," Pippa said.

William bent, resting his hands on his knees until his face came level with Elinor's frown. "I believe you promised to introduce me to your magically delicious pear tarts, Miss Mackenzie."

Her frown lost its irritated edge. "I know you will like them."

"I hope you are correct. Shall we?" He stood, bending his elbow and offering it to Elinor like he was a gentleman taking her on a stroll. She grinned and placed her tiny hand on his arm, and they took off toward the food table. Music built behind them as a drum added its steady beat to the violin, and people clapped and hurrah'd the musicians—their friends.

William stood before the table, a pear tart in his hand and an exaggerated, anxious look on his face. Pippa followed them, standing between them, as Elinor giggled again.

"You simply eat it," she said around a crumbly bite of pastry. Evidence of the treat clung to her mouth and over her chin. Perhaps it was not unreasonable that Pippa would have had a crumb on her lip after all.

Her skin burned at the memory, and she fought the rising blush.

"I am trusting you, Miss Mackenzie." William lifted the tart toward Elinor before popping it in his mouth in its entirety. They'd been made small, but not *that* small. Surely it was too much for one man's mouth.

"What do you think of it?" Elinor asked, bouncing on her feet.

William chewed slowly, making exaggerated sounds of enjoying the food. So exaggerated, in fact, that Pippa was absolutely certain he hated it. She fought a smile, and William glanced at her from the side, continuing to chew.

Their eyes locked, and Pippa couldn't contain her amusement. She broke out in a full grin that stretched over her cheeks and deepened the creases near her eyes. William's laughing countenance matched hers, and she crossed her arms over her chest.

"You do not like them, do you?" she asked.

William swallowed visibly and looked about the table as though searching for something to drink. "Well, it *was* a pear tart," he said with the apparent expectation that that was explanation enough.

"Can you really despise them? They are so sweet. Who would not enjoy a small pie the size of a biscuit?"

"Yes, they are sweet," he agreed. "Sweet and wet and . . . granulated."

Pippa laughed, resting her hand on her full stomach.

Elinor shook her head in confusion. "Perhaps you need to try another one."

William's hand rose in a halting expression, and he took a step back. "No, I thank you. I am quite decided in my dislike for that particular fruit."

He winked at Pippa, and her chest tightened. Must he keep doing that?

William glanced over her shoulder and narrowed his gaze, seemingly looking at something in the distance.

Elinor appeared to have tired of their conversation, for she tugged on Pippa's sleeve. "I want to see Fanny."

"I think your mother would prefer if you—"

"I will not go far!" Elinor called, running past them toward a group of girls.

"Stay away from trees!" Pippa yelled back. She faced William again, and he was as still as a marble statue, his blinking eyes the only proof of life. "Mr. Blakemore?"

He didn't respond. Pippa stepped before him, suppressing her concern. "William, has something happened?"

His eyes flicked down at her, worry lacing their clear blue depths. William said nothing but stepped around her and walked into the crowd.

Pippa wasn't sure what had frightened him, but one thing was perfectly clear: William was terrified of something.

CHAPTER 12

*A*insworth was here somewhere.

William wasn't precisely sure where, for he'd followed the man into the crowd and Ainsworth had disappeared like a specter on a moonless night. The town had shown up in full force to support the Blakemore men, joining them for the welcoming feast if they were not already helping in the fields, but even considering that, there were not so many people here as to make entirely losing a man possible. If he'd seen Ainsworth—and he was absolutely certain he had—then he was still around.

William approached the group of older men sitting around on crates and makeshift chairs.

"Father," William said, bending down to speak into his ear. "I saw Ainsworth."

His father's shoulders stiffened, but his smile remained perfectly situated. "It was a trick of the light."

"No, I truly think—"

Father laughed loudly, slapping William on the back. "Too much to drink, dear boy. You might want to slow down."

Was that entirely necessary? He'd only drunk one measly cup

of ale, and no one in the vicinity had heard what he'd said to his father.

"Do you not have others you wish to speak to?" Father said, the lines tight about his mouth. "Get to know these good people, Will. They are the best in all of England."

A round of cheers followed his pronouncement.

Father certainly did not believe his own words, or he would not have lived the last twenty years in Dorset, surely.

"But Father, I think—"

"Go, Will. Meet more of the good people of Collacott." His hard tone had a strong undercurrent of meaning which was not lost on William. If he did not walk away from tonight's festivities with more connections, he would receive a tongue lashing later that night. His father was not pleased with his lack of progress in winning over the people, but he thought he'd done a good enough job.

He was tired of playing games.

William left his father behind. He circled slowly around a group of children playing cup and ball and made his way toward the music. A man played the violin splendidly beside another man beating a steady rhythm on a crude drum. The group dancing in the center of the small clearing consisted of an array of all ages, and William stepped back, raking his gaze over the groups of people, searching for the familiar wavy hair and freckled nose belonging to Ainsworth.

The intruder hadn't been wearing any sort of uniform, as far as William had been able to tell, but it was him all the same. Ainsworth had promised to make them pay for what Roger did, and it would appear that he had finally found them. He'd come to collect.

Roger sidled up to William, crossing his arms over his chest as mischief danced in his eyes. "They've almost convinced me to enjoy being in Collacott."

William continued to search the crowds, distracted. He

would not be able to rest easily until he found Ainsworth and whoever he brought with him. Surely he had not come alone.

"William?"

He glanced at Roger. "Oh? Was it the food or the dancing?"

"Neither. I think it was their complete willingness to do all the work for us today and then feed us." He grinned. "I could get quite used to this."

William swallowed his disgust. "You hadn't planned to work the field or cook your own dinner this evening, so I'm not exactly sure what you were saved from doing."

Roger looked at him sharply.

William should warn Roger. The man clearly hadn't seen Ainsworth himself or he would be much more worried and far less snappy. The words quickly died on his lips when their cook, Lily, approached with a shy smile.

"Good evening, Miss Burke," William said, bowing. He couldn't speak of Ainsworth while they had an audience.

She curtsied to them both. "Will you be dancing gentlemen, or do you prefer to watch from afar?"

The poor woman was absolutely begging to be asked for a dance, and William hesitated. He liked her well enough, but if he danced this evening, it wasn't Lily he wanted to dance with.

It was Pippa.

"I could be persuaded," Roger said with a rakish lilt to his words. "What inducement could you offer? An extra pudding this week, perhaps?"

Lily's cheeks bloomed with bright spots of color, a smile stretching over her lips. "I could bake a batch of ginger biscuits this week, I suppose."

"In that case, would you care to dance, Miss Burke?" Roger asked, stepping forward and offering his hand.

Lily looked between Roger and William, her smile widening before she laughed and accepted. They walked toward the dancers in the clearing, and William returned to his hunt for Ainsworth.

If the revenue man had just arrived in Collacott and made his way directly to Ravenwood Cottage, he could not have chosen a better time to arrive than now, when their home was overrun with people. Though the longer William's search came up empty, the more he grew to doubt his own eyes. But no, he'd seen the man clear as day. He was here somewhere.

Or perhaps he was no longer *here* precisely. Could Ainsworth have slipped away so quickly? He did not have reason to hide from them, surely.

He had the law on his side. He *was* the law.

A sickening lurch roiled William's stomach, fear tightening the coil within him. They weren't safe here anymore.

The dancers shifted while a new set formed, and William caught sight of Pippa across the clearing. Her face came in and out of view as people walked between them, and he shifted his position to see her better. She nodded along to what an older woman was saying to her, her gaze focused and intent, listening in a thoughtful way.

William must have been staring, for Pippa turned her head and caught his eye, and he couldn't help but smile. She dipped her neck, a shy smile crossing over her lips.

He was relieved that she hadn't ignored him completely after his impoliteness earlier when he'd walked away from her. Seeing Ainsworth had been a frightening surprise he hadn't been prepared for; he was fairly certain he hadn't even bid her farewell. The shock had been great, but Pippa didn't know that. She must think him the rudest sort.

William circled around the dancers, and Pippa studiously avoided his gaze as he approached. He caught her eyes repeatedly, only for her to shift away quickly as though she hadn't been watching him. But she had. And he loved it.

"Good evening," William said, sketching a soft bow. "Again."

THE SMUGGLER OF CAMDEN COVE

Pippa watched him with mild confusion. She gestured to the woman she was speaking to. "Are you familiar with Mrs. Nibley?"

"No, I don't believe I've had the pleasure of an introduction yet," William said, bowing to the matronly woman.

She tittered, dipping in a soft curtsy. "I knew your father when he was a lad. In fact, I remember when you were just a lad, too. Though I cannot recall quite how long ago that was." Mrs. Nibley pressed her finger to her chin. "The years all start to run together, you see."

"I would supply you with that information, but I fear it will age me dramatically. I'd much rather pretend I am young."

Mrs. Nibley laughed, and he'd managed a smile from Pippa. Success coursed through his body at that small win. He could not imagine how wonderful it would feel to obtain a *large* win from Pippa. A laugh or some such thing.

Mrs. Nibley tsked. "Compared to me, you are quite young, Mr. Blakemore. Surely you could not be more than five and twenty."

William cleared his throat, glancing at the people around them. "I believe another dance is beginning shortly, and I wanted to ask if you would be interested in partnering me, Miss Sheffield?"

"She loves to dance," Mrs. Nibley said. "I'm certain she would much prefer dancing to listening to an old woman chatter on."

William looked at the lady in question, raising his eyebrows in surprise. "Is that so?"

"I will not speak to which of the two options I prefer," Pippa said, giving Mrs. Nibley a reproachful look, "but I do feel I must dance now, or I risk offending our newest neighbor."

"We cannot have that," Mrs. Nibley said in all seriousness.

William shook his head. "No, I dare say we cannot." He

offered his arm and Pippa took it, wrapping her hand around his forearm.

"Have I saved you from a most laborious conversation?" he asked, tilting his head toward her and lowering his voice.

"No."

She did not grant him more of a response, despite his quiet patience, and they joined the group preparing to dance a lively reel. William divided his attention between Pippa and watching the crowds for Ainsworth's familiar face, but was fruitless on the last count. It appeared that the revenue man was gone, which was equal parts nerve-inducing and a relief.

The music soared around them, and William threw himself into the dance, finding that he enjoyed it far more than he would have expected. Pippa danced without reserve, performing the reel with enthusiasm and little care for what others might think of her.

The effect was absolutely dazzling. William had difficulty keeping his eyes off her, which resulted in more than one misstep. The dance lengthened, the music continuing on and on as the dancers repeated the steps in rhythm. Pippa caught William's gaze and grinned, her unabashed joy penetrating his reserve until his smile matched hers.

They seemed to be unable to tear their gazes away from one another. Mid-step, Pippa turned the opposite direction she was meant to, colliding directly with William's chest instead of curling away from him. He caught her in his arms and moved back so the dance could continue without them. He tugged Pippa away from the crowd, their chests heaving in time, and she laughed, throwing her head back in unrefined, unabashed humor.

"Tell me that song does come to an end," William said between gasps for air.

"Oh, eventually," Pippa said. "I'm certain we weren't the first couple to quit."

Couple. He and Pippa. William liked the sound of that very much.

She rested her hands on her waist as she drew in deep breaths and walked away from the dancers. William followed her until they'd slipped out of the throng and lingered on the outside of the gathering.

"When I imagined you dancing a Scottish reel on the beach, I had no idea just how accurately my mind had depicted the image."

"Was it everything you hoped it would be?" William asked, unable to help himself. He knew he'd looked a fool, but he'd enjoyed doing so.

"It was even better," Pippa said. She was radiant. The sun fell behind the trees that encased the clearing and darkness slowly descended on them. As though she'd had the same thought, Pippa looked up at the sky. "I need to find my brother-in-law soon."

"And I need to be off to the beach soon."

She gave him an inquisitive look, and he shrugged. "Fishing."

"Were you a fisherman before coming here?"

He was fairly certain there was more to Pippa's question than she let on, and the glowing in his chest dimmed. "I have always been a man of the sea," he said carefully.

She grew still. "A man of the sea? Or a fisherman?"

William should have known that he could not slyly pass Pippa's question. She was much too clever. He wanted to explain himself, but he was lost for words. What could he say to her? That he was a successful smuggler who had for years evaded British law and revenue men and harmlessly provided his people with affordable goods—all the while lining his own pockets? He could not say that, for it was untrue. His work had not been harmless. Men had died. His own *mother* had died. And he was not proud of the things he'd done.

Mac approached them before William could find the right words, and he noticed the tightening around Pippa's eyes and mouth. She was not pleased with him, and it stung, no matter that the cause lay squarely on William's shoulders.

"Are you ready to leave?" Mac asked Pippa. "Mabel has gone home already with Liam and Hope. I've told Winthrop and the others to remain as long as they'd like."

"I am ready."

Mac slapped William on the back. "Welcome to Collacott."

"I cannot adequately thank you for the warm welcome you've given us. Though if your wife is to be believed, the people of Collacott merely used my neediness as an excuse to throw a feast and dance."

"Well, certainly," Mac said. "But don't let Mabel fool you entirely. We are always happy to help our friends."

William's chest warmed and expanded. Friend. He couldn't recall the last time he'd had a friend merely for the sake of it, and not for what they could provide for him. Even Roger was more of an associate than a friend.

It was a shocking discovery to feel how desperately he appreciated Mac's approval. But as quickly as he relished the title of friend, he crashed to the earth in the stark realization that he was severely undeserving of it. He had come to Collacott running away from the law—which had evidently followed him —and had already begun the process of bringing unlawful smuggling to Camden Cove's peaceful shores.

Once Mac—a blasted *Navy* man, for goodness' sake—discovered what William was truly about, he would not be so welcoming. He would undoubtedly regret his ready acceptance of the Blakemore men.

William stepped away from them. He needed to put distance between himself and the Mackenzie family, Pippa included. He could not allow his heart to become entangled in the utopian peace they offered him. Not when it was sure to be short-lived.

"Thank you for your help today, Mac. I owe you a great debt, and I'm glad to pay it the moment you find yourself in need." William could hear the distance in his voice, and he suppressed a wince at Pippa's confused expression.

"I believe you've saved my daughter twice now, Mr. Blakemore. We are certainly even."

"Call me William, and I leave my offer open." With a quick bow, William turned and fled.

CHAPTER 13

*T*he choppy waves splashed against the side of the skiff and rocked William and Roger with their lulling rhythm. He dragged the net from the water with Roger's help and smiled at the plentiful pilchards flopping from within the rope's confines.

"We might not be so awful at this fishing thing after all," Roger said.

William chuckled, taking up an oar to row back to Collacott. "Yes. Perhaps one day we might even find success in more than one net full of fish."

"I doubt we'll be fishing long enough for that to be necessary." Roger looked out over the rocky cliffs that dropped sheer sides down to the water. "Jack will be here soon."

"And we've nowhere to hide the goods."

Roger looked confused. "I thought you dug a pit in the shed."

"I did, but it isn't nearly large enough. My father thinks we ought to find another place to stash the barrels."

Roger's gaze sought the cliffs. "I'll keep an eye out, but it's blasted difficult to see. Could we not take them directly into town?"

"No." William spoke no more, and Roger didn't seem to care, instead watching the cliffs for signs of sea caves while he rowed.

Soon they'd be crossing near Camden Cove, where Jack intended to make the drop in a few days' time, and William couldn't help but comb the beach for sight of Pippa. It was unreasonably late, and he knew he wouldn't find her walking the sandy shore, but that didn't stop him from looking.

He'd beaten such a hasty retreat from her after the feast a few nights before that he was nearly ashamed of himself. But what else could he have done? He needed to keep distance between them or he would hurt her. She was already suspicious if her question had been any clue. *A man of the sea or a fisherman?*

William loved the sea, and he was good at what he did. It didn't take a great deal of skill to row a boat, fill it with barrels, and take them inland. But it did take finesse to keep the towns-people happy so they would look the other way when a drop came in, and it took greasy fingers to slip coin to the revenue men he could entice in such a way.

He loved being on the ocean, or near it. He loved the sound of the waves and the salt in the air.

But he didn't love smuggling.

His feelings were irrelevant, though. He couldn't let his father or Jack down, and Roger was depending on him, too, fool that he was.

"Why can't we take the loot directly into town?"

"Hmmm?" William asked, his mind having traveled to visions of a laughing, dancing Pippa.

"I just want to know why that is not an option. It cuts the need to hide anything."

William knew he'd have to tell Roger about seeing Ainsworth, though he'd hoped to put it off until he could confirm that it was true and not a trick of the light. He didn't want to worry the man if it was unnecessary. The trouble was that he'd gone into Collacott twice since the night of the feast and hadn't seen Ainsworth anywhere. But he was nearly positive it was him, and he would find where Ainsworth was hiding . . . and moreover, *why*.

William cleared his throat. "I believe I saw Ainsworth. He's here."

Roger's eyes widened, the moonlight shining from them as his arms went slack and his oar ceased moving. "Where? When? How many men did he have with him?"

The boat rocked with the waves, undulating up and down in a smooth, rolling motion. "The night of the feast. He slipped away before making himself known, but he was there, I know it. What I do not understand is why he is choosing to hide, and why he came alone."

Roger scrubbed a hand over his face. "What game is he playing?"

"I haven't quite figured it out myself. I hoped to know more before giving you reason to worry. To at least confirm his identity."

Roger's mouth tightened. "We must find a sea cave or dig another hiding place in the shed. If he did not come with a company of men, then . . . well, I'm not sure what that means. But we ought to be careful."

"The shed cannot support another hole, but I'm sure we can find something."

"Shall we row closer to the shores?" Roger asked. It was nearly humorous how willing he was to work when his own neck was on the line.

William agreed, and they moved closer inland.

"It's too blasted dark."

The moonlight wasn't bright enough to see by. Water splashed up the side of the boat again, misting the men. Roger's fear was nearly palpable, edging his motions and tone in clipped nervousness. But if Ainsworth had come to arrest him, surely he would have already done so.

Ainsworth's anger the night his fellow revenue officer died flashed in William's mind. He'd promised to exact his revenge, and William believed him. William felt for the man. He'd lost people he loved as well due to smuggling, and he understood the validity of Ainsworth's anger.

But he loved his family, too, and he valued loyalty. It was his duty to protect Roger and his father in whatever way he could.

"Tomorrow, Roger. We'll find something tomorrow."

CHAPTER 14

*T*he streets of Collacott ran downhill like narrow, cobbled vines and converged at the mouth of the ocean. Pippa stepped down the familiar rocky lane, passing the dark-trimmed houses that ran together along the road. The blue ocean sparkled below her at the base of the hill. The afternoon sun beat down, though its rays could not be felt on the crisp, autumn day.

Pippa waved to Mrs. Nibley, who leaned out her upper story window, hanging wet laundry on a line.

Pippa and Elinor had managed to gather an abundance of pears from their old trees over the previous few days, and quite a few pears sat snugly in her basket now. She pulled the handle higher on her arm and turned the corner sharply at the break in the buildings toward the Burkes' house.

A man stood in the center of the path, looking down at a small book in his hands, and Pippa was forced to pull herself up to avoid running directly into him.

He didn't appear to notice her, and Pippa waited a moment before she cleared her throat. He glanced up, his startled gaze widening.

"Forgive me," Pippa said. She gestured to the dark, painted door behind him. "I'm trying to reach that door."

"Oh, I see." He gave her a wide smile. "No one is home, I'm afraid. I knocked just a few minutes ago."

"Do you need to find the Burkes?"

"Yes." His smile didn't slip, and his gaze turned calculating. "I'm told Mr. Burke is the man to speak to regarding my fishing questions."

"He's likely gone on to Upper Mowstead to deliver last night's load."

The man nodded, rubbing his fingers over his chin. "Do you know when I can expect him to return?"

"I do not, sorry. But I'm certain if you're only after fishing questions, any man in Collacott could answer you."

His fingers stilled on his chin, and his gaze swept over her in a calculating manner. "What of the women? Do you lot know much about the fishermen?"

Fisher*men*? Not fishing? Unease crept into Pippa's stomach and turned it over. The man's beady gaze was fastened on her, and she wished she could peel it off.

She did her best to give him a friendly smile, despite her reservations. "Depends on what you'd like to know."

"Of course. I've been quite rude. Forgive me." He removed his hat and dipped in a bow. His dark, wavy hair thinned on top, though he didn't appear much older than William or even his cousin Roger. "Mr. Ainsworth, ma'am. I've come to inspect the fishing practices of a certain gentleman and his . . . men. Mr. Richard Blakemore, in fact. Are you familiar with the man?"

"Vaguely," Pippa said. Though she knew Mr. Blakemore hadn't fished once since arriving in Collacott—his son and cousin had. "Might I ask what business you have with him?" And furthermore, what sort of business would lead him to question Mr. Burke instead of Black Heart Blakemore himself? It would seem that Pippa had been correct in her initial estimations of this man. He was certainly up to something.

"It is a matter of the law, ma'am. I am not able to say more than that, you understand." Mr. Ainsworth took a small step forward, his thick eyebrows inching closer together. "Do you know much about the Blakemores, ma'am?"

She swallowed, keeping her face impassive. "They are relative strangers, Mr. Ainsworth. I'm not sure anyone in Collacott knows much about them yet."

"Ah, of course." He sent her a wide smile and placed his hat back on his head. "I plan to stay at the White Swan Inn. If you hear of anything untoward, please send word to me there."

He began to walk away and Pippa called to him. "How long do you intend to stay, Mr. Ainsworth?"

He glanced at her over his shoulder. "As long as I need to."

His words sent a lasting chill through Pippa. She wanted to question him further, but her inquiries died on her tongue. He'd left her with more uncertainty, but she didn't know whether William was the one she needed to be wary of, or this Mr. Ainsworth.

Pippa knocked on the Burkes' door and waited, but no answer came. She tried to open it so she could leave the pears inside but was met with resistance. She set the basket on the ground near the door, then turned and left, her mind running down the empty cobblestone road toward the inn. Mr. Ainsworth had mentioned he was with the law, but not in what capacity he served. He wore no uniform, and he had purposefully dismissed her when she did not appear to know anything.

What was his aim?

Pippa slipped between the buildings and back onto the path that led out of town and toward Camden Court. She untied her bonnet strings and slid the offending headwear off, holding it by the ribbons. She wore the thing when in town or other social functions because she knew it was important to Mabel that she look put-together. Indeed, Pippa understood that she represented her sister poorly when she removed her bonnet and allowed her skin to darken, her freckles to increase.

But she couldn't help it. The sun felt warm and comfortable on her skin, and bonnets were such bothersome devices.

Pippa walked the length of the path along the ocean cliff toward her home, her bonnet trailing behind her. She couldn't remove Mr. Ainsworth and his odd questions from her mind and was too distracted to notice Lily until she was an arm's length in front of Pippa.

"What are you doing here?" Pippa asked.

Lily tucked her chin. "I'm walking home, and you are obviously distracted. I called your name when I was there." She gestured behind her. "Are you coming from town?"

Pippa nodded. "I left a basket of pears on your step." She was tempted to ask if Lily knew anything about Ainsworth.

"Mama wasn't home?" Lily's brows scrunched together. "I thought she told me she had enough laundry to keep her busy all day. I'm surprised if she went with Papa to Upper Mowstead."

"*More* laundry?" Pippa dropped her bonnet in her surprise and bent to retrieve it. "Is that typical?"

"No, but Mama has been taking in extra work when she can. The Blakemores have begun sending theirs to her as well. She wants to take Tommy to see another doctor in Melbury."

"Can I not persuade you to allow Mabel to send for Dr. Mason?"

"It hardly matters what I permit. My papa will never allow it, and you know that."

Pippa blew out a frustrated breath. "It isn't charity, Lily."

Lily screwed up her eyes. "We see it differently, I suppose."

"Then I suppose I ought to walk home with you and retrieve those pears I left on your step. You won't be wanting them, surely."

Lily's lips flattened. "You know that is different. An offering from a friend and sharing of your bounty is not the same as paying for medical help. It would be too much a blow to my father's pride."

Pippa tried to gentle her tone. "We don't need to pay Dr. Mason, either. He is a dear friend to the family. We merely need to invite him to visit us. He is far more capable than any man in Melbury, even Dr. Garvey."

Lily's eyes tightened. "Say no more, please. We will not see eye to eye on this."

Pippa suppressed the temptation to stomp her foot in agitation. It wasn't Lily's fault, and Pippa couldn't expect everyone to agree with her, even if she was correct in this matter.

"Besides, if you take the pears home with you, how will I make pear tarts for the Blakemore men?"

"Save your pears for your own family, Lily."

Lily looked irritated. "That isn't very charitable of you."

Pippa wanted to scoff at the irony folded into that statement. "I only meant that they would be wasted otherwise. Mr. Blakemore doesn't like pears. He didn't like Mabel's tarts at the feast."

"Oh." Lily looked out over the sea. "I see."

The air between them was heavy and tense. "Have I done something to upset you?"

Lily shook her head. A blonde tendril came loose from her low knot and she tucked it back behind her ear. "No. I just . . . I do not wish to speak prematurely. I best not say anything at all."

"What has happened, Lily?"

She bit her bottom lip, indecision ripe on her face. "I think I may be falling in love, is all. And I dare to hope he might love me back."

"*Love*, Lily? That is . . ." Pippa swallowed her initial disappointment. Lily had to be speaking of William still. "Are you certain he is not merely a flirt? Have you even known the man long enough to *love* him?"

Lily scoffed. "A man does not look at me in that way or speak such flowery words without intent. He must mean it." She narrowed her blue eyes. "You are the one who told me to hope."

"Surely he does have intent, but is it worthy? Are you certain it is of a good nature?" Pippa wanted to have faith that Lily was not being taken advantage of. But if that were the case and the relationship was legitimate, then William was drawing two women under his spell, and that was a frightening prospect.

Lily sighed. "I should be on my way home." She gave a long-suffering chuckle. "I finished the Blakemores' dinner, and now it seems I ought to be getting started on my own."

"Of course." Pippa pulled her friend in for a hug. Lily walked the pathway toward Collacott, and Pippa watched her go, running the conversation over in her mind. She hadn't meant to give Lily false hope when she'd said that she should know her own worth. If Lily got hurt, it would be Pippa's fault entirely.

A dark mood followed her on the remainder of her walk, matching the gray clouds clinging above the ocean and rolling over the beach. The closer Pippa drew to Camden Court, the more her irritation mounted and grew. Lily was not a silly creature. If she believed herself in love, that a man could possibly love her in return, she must have just cause for thinking so.

Lily would not make herself up to a man she deemed above her station. No, if anything, she would do the opposite for fear of stepping out of line and losing the money she knew her family relied on. She was his servant, for heaven's sake.

William's behavior must be at fault in some way. It was the only explanation that held any merit.

Pippa passed the road that led into Camden Court, quickening her steps so she would not be seen, and continued on toward Ravenwood Cottage. Surely she could visit on the guise of . . . *something* neighborly . . . and deliver a quick, stern warning to leave Lily alone if there was no attachment already. William would hardly be able to look Pippa in the eye and admit to his feelings for Lily without some degree of discomfort. The man was falsely flirting with *one* of them.

She pulled up short on the fork in the path and turned her back on the trail that led into the Blakemore's small grove. Pippa looked out over the gray sky and choppy, dark waves. She'd been so offended by Lily's revelation, but why? Surely it would not have hurt so deeply if Pippa had not believed William to be authentic in his interactions with her.

The turmoil in the ocean reflected the churning of her stomach, and Pippa shut her eyes against the image before her. She had never been the type given to bouts of jealousy, and these feelings for William were every bit as new and foreign as they were dreadful and exciting. Pressing her palm to her midsection, Pippa drew in a clean, salty breath and released it through her nose. She opened her eyes, ready to return home and leave her confrontation with William to another day.

"Miss Sheffield," William called, approaching from the path that led to his house.

Or perhaps she would have that confrontation now.

William's coat was missing, his shirtsleeves rolled up and cravat dangerously loosened, revealing his tanned forearms and throat. Was the man desperate to make this difficult for her?

"Miss Sheffield?" he asked, the question lacing his words and drawing confusion on his brow. "Is something amiss?"

"Of course not," she said brightly. Though her bonnet ribbons would soon be a crumpled mess if she clutched them any tighter.

He lifted an eyebrow. He'd seen through her false assurance. "Now I know something is most definitely not right. What is it?"

"Nothing." Goodness, must her voice sound so high and unnatural?

He opened his mouth as though he meant to speak but closed it again without uttering a word. Resting his hands on his waist, William looked past her. "I was going down to the cove for a bit. Would you care to join me?"

Pippa swallowed hard. This was the opportunity she needed to question him and warn him away from Lily, so why was she having such difficulty forming the words? She supposed it was easier to feign bravado when alone and fuming, but faced with the object of her anger was a whole different thing entirely. It was difficult to think straight when he had a habit of sending her heart into frantic turmoil.

"For a few minutes, perhaps," she finally said, as though she were a busy woman and hadn't planned on going down to the cove already on her own. They turned for the path down to the beach, and William did not offer her his arm, for which she was grateful. She could hardly recall exactly why she was angry with the man, and she was certain that all reason and sense would flee were he to touch her again.

They traveled down to the beach in silence and the steep walls of earth rose around them, cocooning them in the palm of the beach in a false sense of privacy. Pippa hadn't considered the inappropriateness of being alone with William on the beach, and the intimacy of walking the secluded stretch of sand made her pulse pound.

What had she been thinking coming down here with him? What had *he* been thinking to ask it of her?

"You seem troubled," he said. But she did not wish to speak of the things which bothered her. Not yet.

"Do you come down here often?" Pippa asked, needing for him to speak about the mundane. Anything to break the spell.

He looked sheepish. "I do. Is that allowed? I hadn't thought to ask permission from your brother-in-law."

"It is not our land, actually. You are more than welcome on this beach."

"I must admit that I expected to meet you here with more frequency. It has been disappointing, to say the least."

Warmth blossomed in Pippa's chest, and she beat it down, forcing herself to remember Lily. This man was not sincere. His handsome grin was not meant for her alone.

"I'm not sure why my presence would matter." Oh, good heavens. Now she most certainly sounded as though she were begging him to compliment and reassure her. She spoke again quickly. "I only mean that surely you do not come down here with the express purpose of meeting me."

"I would disagree with you but my mother taught me to be more polite."

Pippa stopped walking and faced him, shaking her head. She could not believe the gumption of this man to be so blatant in his flirtations just minutes after leaving Lily's presence and giving her the same treatment. "You do realize that Lily Burke is my closest friend, do you not?"

William looked startled. "Yes. Well, I had assumed you were close to her, at least."

She scoffed. "And still you persist?"

The wind increased, whipping her skirts about her legs as the clouds darkened and the water turned a deep gray.

"What exactly are you referring to, Pippa? In what way am I persisting?"

"My Christian name!" she said, as though this were the very proof she needed. "Your generous flirtations. You cannot honestly believe that I would pursue a man who has given my dearest friend reason to believe herself falling in *love*."

"Love?" His eyes widened and he leaned away from her, as though the words she spoke carried contagion. "Lily?"

"Do you deny that you have flirted with her? That you have given her reason to believe you care for her?"

"Yes. Indeed. Emphatically."

Pippa was surprised by the vehemence of his words. "She is

not a foolish girl, and I'm certain she would not reach this point of her own volition. She must have been encouraged."

"Encouraged by me? She said as much?" For his part, William looked stricken. If he was playing a role, he was doing a remarkable job of it.

"She did." Pippa wanted to believe this man, but she could not put Lily's convictions aside so easily. "She told me not a half-hour ago that she was given reason to believe her love to be returned."

William rested one hand on his hip and ran his other through his hair. "I have been friendly with Lily, but certainly don't think I've given her cause to believe . . ." He looked at Pippa then. "Truly, you must understand. If I did so, it was without intent."

"Then *you* must understand why I cannot take you for your word. How am I to trust a gentleman who professes to not know when he has flirted excessively with a poor young woman?"

"*Poor young woman*, Pippa? You speak as though you are matronly, and I cannot imagine you in such a role."

"I am wonderful with children, I thank you."

"Ah, yes. You must enjoy climbing trees with them and prancing through rock pools."

Pippa's smile faltered. Did William see her this way? A joke? A young child? Perhaps that was why he was so quick to banter with her.

"Did I offend you?" He stepped closer. "I meant it as a compliment, believe it or not."

"To be quite frank, I'm not certain what to believe right now."

William hesitated, looking down into her eyes. He was so close, she could smell his woodsy, warm scent, and she wanted to inhale deeply. "If I've given Lily reason to believe I have developed a fondness for her, it was unconsciously done. I assure you,

Pippa, there is only one woman who I think about, and it is most certainly not Lily."

That did not mean the one woman he thought about was Pippa, either. She looked toward the ocean, desperately wishing for something to anchor her.

William's gloveless fingers rested lightly against her jaw, turning her to look at him, forcing her to meet his eyes—though she turned her head quite willingly. "If I was unclear, Pippa, I was referring to you."

CHAPTER 15

*T*o say that the air had swooped from her lungs in one swift blow was doing it mildly. William's hand remained lightly touching her jaw, as though he hovered on the edge of a cliff and hadn't yet decided to jump. She turned her head into his hand more fully, reveling in the warmth his skin provided.

"Am I a complete ninny to believe that you might hold a similar regard for me?" he asked.

Pippa crashed back to the earth swiftly. Could she believe this man? She wanted to, undoubtedly, but that did not mean she should. She stepped back from his hold, and his hand dropped to his side. "Whether or not it was done unconsciously, Lily believes her feelings to be returned. What sort of friend would I be to admit to such a thing when faced with that truth?"

"An honest one."

Pippa laughed. "You cannot wrap this situation in flowery words and make it better. It is dratted uncomfortable, regardless of how you frame it."

"Despite your protestations, you've done nothing but give me reason to hope." His eyes softened. "Put me out of my misery and be forthright."

"No."

William's laugh ripped through the howling wind. "No? Whyever not?"

"I must speak to Lily first." Despite her pretended bravado, Pippa very much enjoyed the way he looked at her now, and it took a great deal of reserve to hold her ground.

"Very well." He seemed to sober further. "I suppose I ought to speak to her, as well."

She swallowed a scoff. "That is likely a good idea."

Thunder sounded in the distance, and William looked up as though seeing the incoming storm for the first time. "We should both be getting home."

"Have you not stood on the beach during a storm? It is a majestic thing to behold."

His gaze slid to her. "I should think it a dangerous thing."

"There is that, too."

William smiled, reaching for her hand, and she let him take it. "Let us get you to safety before you find a way to somehow become stuck in the storm, and I am forced to rescue you."

"Yes, because our relationship thus far has been rife with you rescuing me," she said drily.

"I suppose not, but I wouldn't wish to begin that trend today."

He hadn't saved *her*, but he had come to the rescue of Elinor on more than one occasion. He had a good heart, he'd proven that much already. The way he'd hastened down to the beach when Elinor had screamed showed exactly what kind of man William was. The sort who ran to help.

Pippa allowed him to tug her along, his large hand wrapped around hers. She felt warm and safe in his hold and wished the climb up to the road would last forever. "Can I ask you a question?"

He looked back at her with curiosity. "Yes."

"Why do you not wear a coat?"

William screwed his eyebrows together. "Stupidity. It is really quite cold out."

They reached the road, and William gestured to her bonnet, which threatened to fly away in the wind, and she clutched the ribbons tighter so it would not escape. "My turn. Why do you not wear your bonnet?"

"Because I love freckles and tanned skin, of course."

William nudged her with his shoulder. "Truly."

"I am not opposed to either of those things, regardless of what Mabel thinks Society approves of. In truth, though, I find bonnets uncomfortable. When I wear them too long they give me headaches."

He nodded. "For what it is worth, I love your dash of freckles and find your tanned skin beautiful."

Warmth stole up her cheeks, and Pippa tore her gaze from William's insistent one. "Thank you, sir."

"That was a sincere compliment, Pippa."

"You take such liberties with my name," she said, challenging him.

A wide, gleaming grin spread over his lips. "I'm afraid it is no longer intentional."

She liked to know that he thought of her in that way. She had thought of him as William since first meeting him. But to give him her express permission now was making an exclamation about their relationship that she was not ready for, not until she'd spoken with Lily.

He looked at her with a questioning gaze, and she ignored it.

Light rain fell on her unadorned nose. "I really must be on my way home."

"Of course." William seemed reluctant to release her, and

she tugged her hand free from his. Cold air swept in and chilled the skin that William had warmed.

"Good evening, then."

"Yes," she agreed, stepping away. "Good—oh! I forgot." Pippa halted and turned back to face him, slightly surprised that he had not moved away at all. He remained standing where she'd parted from him, his feet firmly planted and hands clasped lightly in front of him. He seemed heedless of the rain dampening his shirt and falling over his hair. "I met a man today in Collacott who was asking about your father's fishing. Or, at least I think—"

William stepped toward her swiftly. "Who was it?"

She paused only briefly before answering, surprised by his reaction. "He told me his name was Mr. Ainsworth, and he was with the law. He did not tell me in what capacity he served, however. And he wore no uniform."

"Blast." William glanced up, and she detected what appeared to be fear in his eyes. "What did he wish to know?"

Unease gripped her. "He was hoping to question Mr. Burke, but no one was home. He asked if I knew anything about your father, that was all."

"What did you tell him?"

"I told him that I know nothing. It is the truth." She searched his worried eyes. "William, are you in some sort of trouble?"

He glanced up quickly. "Me, no. But . . . I really should not say more than that. It is better if you are ignorant."

"Better for whom?"

A smile ticked up his lips.

Pippa did not relent. "If you are in trouble, Mac can help. He knows a lot of people and is generally well-liked and respected."

William's smile tightened. "I will keep that in mind."

Rain fell in earnest now, wetting William's sleeves until they clung to his defined arms. She struggled to tear her gaze away.

Why had she offered her brother-in-law's assistance when she did not know the first thing about the nature of the Blakemores' trouble? Did not the past prove that the Blakemore men cared little for the law? *Black Heart Blakemore* himself had moved into the cottage out of the blue with little explanation after two decades' absence.

But how could she judge this man and his family for smuggling when her own father purchased smuggled goods?

Uncertainty nipped at her heels like a poorly trained hound; she looked into William's light blue gaze and found the anchor she'd been searching for over the last hour. There, nestled deep within the chocolate irises and concern, was a steadiness that held her feet securely to the ground and sustained her. Pippa knew not why William had that effect on her. She only knew of the power that swam through her limbs and straight into her heart. Reason aside, she trusted this man.

But she wasn't certain she should.

"Did he happen to say anything else?" William asked.

"Only that he is staying at the White Swan."

William rubbed his chin, his eyes thoughtful. "Will you tell me if you see him again? If you hear anything else?"

Pippa nodded. "I can do more than that if you will but trust me, though. I—"

"No." His voice was as solid as the rocks which sat stalwart in the middle of the rising tide, immovable and strong. "It is not for lack of trust, Pippa. Your safety is important to me, and I will not be responsible for embroiling you in this."

"Surely nothing can come of my knowing exactly what sort of trouble *this* is."

He shook his head, but his gaze did not move from her face. Pippa felt a pull toward William with an invisible force. She walked the three steps back to him and paused close enough to see the light and dark flecks of blue in his eyes and the flaring of his nostrils. He was so still, but his inner turmoil was evident in his unsteady breathing.

"Have I done something to anger you?" she asked.

He tucked his chin, clearly taken by surprise. "No."

"Your nose is reacting as if you are mad."

A smile split his mouth, and he chuckled. Whatever had made William temper his breathing a moment before had now fled enough to relax his shoulders. He reached for her cheek and brushed a lock of hair out of her eyes, but the wind was a stronger force than he, and her hair was soon dancing along her forehead again. William's large hands wiped over her temples, moving the hair and holding it back as he framed her face with his hands. "When will this blasted wind cease?"

"Never, of course. Welcome to the Devonshire coast, sir."

He chuckled again, and his gaze dropped to her lips.

Good heavens, Pippa had never felt such deep anticipation and the dropping of her stomach simultaneously. She pulled her lips in-between her teeth, and William's eyes snapped up to meet hers.

The rain continued to fall and William released her face, stepping back and drawing in a deep breath. "You will be at church tomorrow?"

"Yes, and I believe you are coming to dinner following the service."

He gave one nod. "Until tomorrow."

Pippa's gaze was drawn to the stormy ocean again. "You do not intend to fish tonight, do you?"

William looked up sharply. "Why do you ask?"

"It will be too dangerous, I fear."

"No," he said, smiling. "I do not intend to fish." He swallowed hard and looked toward the sea again, and Pippa turned to leave. Her gown was soaked through, and if she did not hurry to dry off and warm her body, she was certain to catch a cold. Not that she was terribly worried about that, but she didn't want anything to get in the way of the Blakemores coming to dinner.

"Good evening, fair Pippa," William called.

She lifted her hand in acknowledgment but continued to hurry toward Camden Court as the rain fell in earnest and a smile danced on her lips.

CHAPTER 16

*W*illiam drew the drapes back against the rainy sky and turned to face his father where he was seated in his customary chair near the fire. The storm had remained mild, though present, and it fostered unease in William's gut.

"I'm not sure it is a good idea to go out on the ocean tonight."

"It is perfect," Roger said. "I was having a pint in town just this afternoon and heard others complaining. No one plans to fish tonight. We are in the clear."

"They do not plan to fish because of the lack of moon or because of the storm?"

Roger shrugged. "Both, I gather."

"Believe it or not, that does not make me feel more at ease."

"We can't let Jack down," Father said, a finality in his tone that grated on William. The very reason he was willing to participate in their venture tonight was because he couldn't let his brother down—not until he made sure Jack was prepared to continue on without William's help. But were their lives not more important than leaving Jack to manage the contraband for another day or so? Though that would be dangerous, too.

William's temper flared. "So we ought to die in order to make sure his stores are delivered? I cannot imagine a soul from Collacott willing to go out with us tonight."

Father's face hardened. "If you'd put more of an effort into winning over the men, we would have more."

"More? So we do have some?" He chose to ignore the pointed dig at his lackluster efforts. He knew he should have tried harder, but he was tired of using people, of charming them for the sole purpose of winning them over to his side. It was an important feature of his old position, for he couldn't expect anyone to turn their backs to his smuggling and pretend they were ignorant of his law-breaking activities unless they benefited from it or approved of him personally. But Collacott felt different. William wanted to forge genuine relationships here, not charm people into liking him so they wouldn't report on him to the revenue men.

Silence sat in the small, damp cottage. William pled for patience and moved to sit near his father and the fire. The warmth from the flames ate away at the chill clinging to his clammy skin. He'd changed out of his wet things, but the cold had lingered. "What men have already agreed to help?"

"John Caney and his nephew, Samuel."

"What about the other bloke?" Roger asked, biting into the pie Lily had left for their supper. "The cook's father."

The *cook's* father? Roger could not even do her the decency of recalling her name? "Mr. Burke?"

"Yes, that's the one," Roger said.

Father looked at the fire. "I'm not sure if he'll come."

William's body froze. Hadn't Pippa told him that she'd met Ainsworth after he knocked on Burke's door? "Why aren't you sure?"

Silence met his question, and William did his best to tamp

down his frustration. When would his father learn to trust him with the things that were important? If William didn't know Father's entire scheme, he could not adequately prepare for things not going according to plan.

Adversely, he'd remained undecided about whether or not telling Father of Ainsworth again was worth the effort when he hadn't believed William the first time, but now he had no choice.

"Ainsworth was in Collacott today questioning the people about our habits. He went to Burke's door, but—"

Father sat up. "What did Burke tell him?"

"Nothing. The man wasn't found at home. He was likely off selling his fish in Upper Mowstead."

Father visibly relaxed, and it only irked William further. "Do you not see the danger in our going out tonight? Ainsworth is *here*. The man is desperate to make us pay." Lightning flashed outside as though the sky were helping to prove his point, and William pointed to the window. "If Ainsworth doesn't lock us up, the sea certainly will."

"We're smugglers, Son. Danger is part of the gig."

That attitude once excited and buoyed William, but no more. "I don't wish to have any part of this."

Roger took another bite of his pie. "Then don't come."

"He'll come," Father growled. He turned his frown on William. "He's a Blakemore. And Blakemores don't leave their men behind."

"None of us would be left behind if we all chose to—"

"*Enough*, Will. I was speaking of Jack."

Ah, yes. Jack. Try as he might, William couldn't think of a reason good enough to convince his father to leave Jack without a way to offload his smuggled goods. Apparently their safety was not a good enough reason. If tonight was going to continue as planned, William had no choice but to help. Father had been correct on that score: William wouldn't leave his brother in a bind.

"I'll help this time for Jack's sake, but it is my last."

Father looked at him shrewdly but didn't argue.

William leaned forward and rested his elbows on his thighs, drawing closer to the hearth in the hopes that his body would warm quicker. He had two hours before it was time to venture out. Perhaps if he prayed hard enough, the weather would mellow and Ainsworth would stay far, far away.

CHAPTER 17

*E*very muscle William possessed clenched tightly against the freezing onslaught of rain. He pressed forward, rowing toward the blinking light swaying in the distance and cursing his brother's name under his breath. Great waves splashed against their boat, rocking them back. For every foot he and his men gained toward Jack's ship, it felt like they lost two more.

"Blasted ship doesn't appear to be growing any closer," Roger hollered over the wind and rain.

"Careful," John replied. "You don't want to wake Mac."

"He won't wake Mac from here," Samuel Caney said, turning confused eyes on his uncle. "Mac's house is too far away for that."

William looked over his shoulder to where Camden Court sat, surrounded by trees and hidden mostly from view. It was too dark to make it out entirely, but the darkness shrouding the estate was comforting all the same. The very last thing William needed was for the navy man to catch them in the midst of their illegal escapades.

John shook his head. "You can't know what carries on the wind. It's best to be cautious."

William agreed with John, but he was fairly certain no one would hear them from the beach. If the wind drowned their voices from being able to reach one another easily, surely they were safe from being overheard by someone far back on the shore.

"Row harder, men," William commanded, pulling at his oar handle with all the strength he could muster. The lantern his brother had lit to signal his sloop bobbed further away, and William was growing anxious. "Come on now, one last push."

They heaved and rowed in time as William counted out the rhythm of the oars. The forward motion felt like sludging through mud instead of water, but they pressed forward and slowly approached Jack's ship. It was too dark to see much, but Jack's face was lit up by the lantern he held, and William couldn't help but feel relieved and glad to see his reckless brother.

"Took you long enough," Jack called. Rain fell lightly around him, causing a hazy glow around the lantern light. It made the blasted devil look like something of an angel.

"The storm hasn't helped much," William called back. Rain sluiced down his neck and chilled him. His boat rocked widely, and he swung to the side, catching himself on the bench.

Jack seemed to search the sea beyond William, forcing him to look over his shoulder again. Ainsworth hadn't followed them, had he?

"Where are the rest of your men?" Jack called.

"This is it."

Jack didn't bother hiding his surprise. "We better be moving or we'll be here all night."

Jack's crew formed a line down the rope ladder and proceeded to fill William's boat with the first load of barrels. They rowed back toward the beach to relieve the load, their chests heaving and limbs aching. It was the first of at least three trips between Jack's sloop and the beach, and William had a feeling he was going to sleep long into the morning. If he made it home unscathed.

"Hurry, men," Roger called, jumping from the boat and carrying the first barrel to the cart that William's father had resting on the beach. Father sat on the driver's seat, prepared to drive away when it was fully loaded.

William struggled to put Pippa from his mind; he felt guilty breaking the law in Camden Cove. It may not belong to Pippa's family by law, but William had considered it Pippa's beach since he first found her in the rock pools with her niece and nephew.

The longer they worked, the more the rain appeared to recede. It was a blessed thing that by the time they loaded the final barrel of brandy into their boat, the rain had ceased completely. William hovered on the rope ladder, having climbed it to help lower barrels of sugar and brandy down to his men. He descended from his brother's sloop to reach his own measly boat, holding tightly to the unsteady rope.

Jack called down, hanging over the railing. "I'll be seeing you in a week, and I'll have twice the loot. Be sure to have triple the men, at least," he said. "And another boat or two."

William bit out a curse. He didn't *want* to be in charge of another drop. He'd agreed to this for the sake of Jack and their father but meant for this to be an isolated situation. He clung to the ladder, the rope digging into his gloved hands. "I'm not sure if that's a good idea. Have you spoken to Father about this?"

Jack lifted his eyebrows, his face glowing orange from the lantern light. "It sounds like it's *you* who needs to have a talk with Father."

Great. Just great. "We don't have the men," William called up, irritated.

"Find them," Jack replied. "There certainly weren't nearly enough today."

William didn't bother to respond but focused on climbing down the slick ladder without slipping. He reached the boat, but it wouldn't remain near enough to make the transfer easy, despite the rope tethering it to Jack's sloop. Huge waves, no doubt fed by the storm, sloshed the small boat about as though his men were a pair of dice in a player's cup and made it difficult for William's shoe to find purchase on the rim.

"Make a jump for it," Roger called, holding on to the side of the boat as he jostled about.

William looked to the dark, fathomless ocean below as he dipped with the swaying boat. He'd seen it swallow men on calmer nights. Was he willing to take the risk? Even skilled swimmers—and he counted himself among them—could not always fight raging waves and win. His gaze sought the beach, and he noticed a light bobbing along the top of the cliff, hazy and blurred from the moisture clinging to the air. It was far too late in the night—or early in the morning, more accurately—for anyone to stroll along the lane.

Surely that had to be Ainsworth. Which meant they needed to get to shore, hide, and give Jack a chance to get away.

Looking down at the boat, William swallowed his last bit of reserve and jumped.

CHAPTER 18

*P*ippa awoke with a niggling in the back of her mind that all was not well. She did not know why she felt so afraid, but she wasn't about to ignore the sensation pulling at her belly and telling her to wake up.

She crossed the room to the window and pulled back the drapes, glancing out over the ocean. Rain on the glass panes made it impossible to see anything but the faint orange glow of a lantern somewhere in the distance. But not just anywhere—someone was out on a boat in the cove, which could really only mean one thing on a night like tonight.

Smugglers.

Pippa dressed simply, throwing her heavy scarlet cloak over her haphazard outfit and cinching it tight. Rain pattered softly against the windowpane, and she brought her hood up to cover her head.

It was easy to sneak down her creaky stairs and into the dark night without detection. Pippa knew the creaks and groans of the old house well, and though it was a delicate dance to reach the door quietly, it was one she did proficiently. If Mabel knew how often Pippa had snuck out to watch the sunrise or walk the beach alone, she wouldn't be pleased. It was harmless—Pippa had never before encountered another soul on her solitary walks before the Blakemores moved to Collacott. But tonight was different.

According to the long-case clock she'd passed in the corridor on her way outside, it was half past three in the morning. A far cry from a sunset or sunrise.

The faint noises of men hollering to one another floated on the wind, but Pippa could see no one; the lack of moon in the sky bathed the cove in heavy darkness and she'd not brought a lantern with her for fear of being seen. She snuck around the trees that protected the drive up to Camden Court but drew up quickly when a lantern bobbed not fifteen feet ahead of her on the lane, inland toward Collacott. Whoever it was, they were likely coming from town and heading toward the beach.

Pippa drew between the trees and watched the light bob closer, slowly revealing the man who carried it. Mr. Ainsworth approached, wearing all black from his hat to his boots. Why was he out so late and with such a look of determination on his furrowed brow? He marched on as though with a purpose, and Pippa waited until he was past her lane and ahead by a good distance before sneaking behind and following him in the darkness.

He nearly reached the turnoff which led down to Camden Cove when he paused on the pathway, and Pippa felt suddenly exposed. There were no more trees out here to cover her, and if Mr. Ainsworth turned around and marched her direction, she would have nowhere to hide. She could make a run for the wood that wrapped around Camden Cove, but not before she would be seen. The sudden foolishness of her impulsive behavior dawned on her, and a fissure of fear ran through her limbs.

The man waited a moment longer, looking out over the ocean. He held the lantern before him as if that would allow him to better see the inky, black water beneath a partially cloudy sky.

Pippa followed his gaze out to the ocean, and her heart kicked into a gallop. There, just beyond the mouth of the cove, was a ship. It wasn't too large, by any means, but she could see the outline as clear as if it had been a moon or star-filled night. The voices she thought she'd heard earlier were clearer now that she was free of the cover of trees, but still she could not discern what they were saying. The sounds were faint, carried on the wind, and she was certain they were coming from that ship.

Smuggling. Just as she'd suspected.

Mr. Ainsworth appeared indecisive. He watched the ship, and Pippa watched him. It *had* to be the Blakemore men out on the water, and if Pippa wasn't mistaken, this man was not on their side.

Where did Pippa fall in this? Whose side would she be on? She hadn't been included in or even informed of William's plans, despite speaking with him earlier that day. Had he kept this from her because he couldn't trust her? That rankled. He'd mentioned her safety, but Pippa couldn't see how a little knowledge of the situation would have been unsafe.

Mr. Ainsworth was with the law—in some capacity, though it was unclear precisely how—and if he caught the men down there in the midst of carrying smuggled goods onto English soil, the Blakemore men would hang. He acted alone, though, which sent a niggle of uncertainty down her spine. If he was an exciseman, would he not have others with him? Surely they would not have sent one man on his own to arrest a group of smugglers.

Something did not add up.

Mr. Ainsworth reached into his coat and pulled out a pistol, the gray metal gleaming beneath his torch. Pippa's heart sped, her breath coming in shallow gusts. The man had a gun; this changed everything.

Mr. Ainsworth stepped forward as if he intended to climb the pathway down to the beach, and Pippa acted before she had time to adequately think through her decision or devise a plan.

She followed him down to the beach, light on her feet, and picked up a heavy piece of driftwood the size of her arm.

She'd never seen a lawman act in such a tricky manner, creeping about and solitary. The lawmen she was familiar with brandished their authority with pride. Mr. Ainsworth walked forward awkwardly on the sand, his gaze trained on the small boat heading their direction. It was the precise size and shape of the Blakemores' fishing boat.

Pippa kept to the shadows behind him, creeping along and keeping a watch on the law man and the smugglers.

Whatever was going on here between Mr. Ainsworth and the Blakemores, it wouldn't end well with a gun involved. But if Pippa could distract Mr. Ainsworth long enough for the Blakemores to get away, she could warn them to steer clear of this beach in the future. Her breathing increased. Fleeting indecision left as quickly as it had arrived. All she needed to do was remove the gun.

Pippa crept behind Mr. Ainsworth and lifted the heavy, dense branch high in the air. She would hit him in the arm, knock his gun to the ground, and—

Mr. Ainsworth started to turn toward Pippa, and she panicked. She brought the branch down swiftly, and it collided with his head. His hat flew forward, rolling on the sand and toward the surf, and Mr. Ainsworth crumpled to the ground. His lantern flew to the side, the light extinguishing in the oncoming wave.

Remorse filled her at once, and she dropped the wood, falling to her knees to roll Mr. Ainsworth onto his back. He was heavier than she imagined someone so lanky to be, and it took a few rocking efforts before she was able to get Mr. Ainsworth onto his back, his face up. His eyes were closed, but she pressed her palm to his chest and felt it rise and fall beneath her touch. Sweet relief fell over her, and Pippa closed her eyes, sending up a prayer of gratitude that she had not deeply hurt the man. Or, so she hoped.

She felt along his head but didn't meet with a wet, sticky substance. He was certain to have a large, swollen bump in the morning, but she hoped that was the worst of it.

And where was the gun?

The sound of water splashing drew her attention to the ocean, and she made out the shapes of men climbing from the boat and stomping through the waves. They created a chain, passing and carrying barrels from the boat to the wagon waiting nearby as one man held a rope to anchor the boat in the tumultuous water. She hadn't before noticed the wagon, but she could now see that it was overflowing with barrels the size of baby Liam, with a man in the driver's seat.

"Where'd he go?" someone called.

"Don't know," another said. "The light went out a few minutes ago."

Pippa froze. Did she step forward now and reveal herself or hide? She couldn't leave Mr. Ainsworth without ensuring that he was well, but she wasn't sure getting caught by this group was wise either, not when she hadn't yet heard William's voice.

"Find him," another voice said; it was too dark to see, but it *could* have been William.

Her choice was made for her when a figure approached, nearing the place Pippa knelt beside Mr. Ainsworth's unconscious body.

"Here," she said, gathering his attention before he could step on her. The man jumped, startled. "Mr. Ainsworth is right here. Is that who you were looking for?"

"Miss Sheffield?" the man asked, disbelieving, and she could see him well enough now to make out his identity. John Caney looked back at her, his eyes dark and beady beneath the moonless sky. His hat was missing, and his hair appeared rumpled and wet.

"Good evening, Mr. Caney," she said pleasantly.

"What . . . I do not understand." He gestured to the prone man beside her. "Who is that?"

"Mr. Ainsworth," she repeated.

Another man approached, and Pippa rose to her full height, grateful to see William. Though she could not help but be offended that he would admit people of Collacott—*her* people—into his schemes, yet he would not so much as tell her of them taking place. She could have helped. Clearly she made an excellent lookout. Unintentional as it had been.

William's eyes were hard, glittering. "What happened?"

"Nothing. He merely . . . fell." Her explanation was weak, and William would undoubtedly see directly through it. "Hurry, all right? You've not got much time. He could awaken at any moment."

"He is alive then?" William asked.

Pippa suppressed her gall at the very question. "*Of course* he's alive. But he won't remain asleep forever. If I were you, I would beat a hasty retreat while you still can."

William shook his head.

"Will?" Mr. Caney asked.

He sighed and brought his hand up to his face. It was too dark to see clearly, the night was lit by very few stars, but she could make out William pinching the bridge of his nose in frustration. It was ridiculous that he was so put out, honestly. She had done him a massive favor.

"You heard her." William sighed heavily. "He won't remain out for long, and we really ought to avoid being caught."

"Right." Mr. Caney jogged back toward the boat to help unload the remaining barrels. Clouds shifted above them, revealing more stars, and subsequently more light. Though Pippa still could not discern whether William was grateful or annoyed by her presence.

He stepped closer, and her heart picked up speed, but he

passed her and crouched beside Mr. Ainsworth. After ensuring that the man was indeed alive, or whatever it was William was doing, he looked up at her. "What are you doing here, Pippa?"

"Saving your hide. You're quite welcome for that. He had a gun, William. A *gun*. Though I can't find it."

He stood, resting his hands on his waist. "Go on, now. Get home. This is dangerous, and you shouldn't be here."

"But you should?"

He scoffed. "I haven't a choice. You do. Now get on home."

The very idea that he felt he could tell her what to do rose the stubborn beast within her breast, and Pippa, though she had quite longed for her warm bedchamber a moment ago, was decidedly *not* leaving yet. "I will remain until I can ascertain that Mr. Ainsworth has not been seriously injured."

"I will see to that."

"You should see to your illegal contraband, I rather think, and quickly at that. Or this law man is bound to awaken and get precisely whatever it is he came here for."

William swore mildly.

"What sort of law man is he, exactly?" she pressed. "He wouldn't happen to be an exciseman, would he?"

William leaned closer. "Go home, Pippa."

Her gaze shifted to Ainsworth and back. "No."

He grunted. "Is your safety really not . . ." He expelled a breath. "Then watch over him if you wish. I am going to help my men." He strode away, leaving her with a racing heart and a thread of annoyance. Her *safety*? The only man who would do her harm was unconscious on the sand before her, and it was her fault. The effrontery to call the others *his men* when they were undoubtedly Collacott men grated on her nerves.

Pippa sat in the sand beside Mr. Ainsworth, watching the tide as best she could to ensure it did not reach them, and fighting concern for the man's wellbeing. She'd never hit a person before, especially not over the head with a branch, and guilt filled her heavily.

Dark, shadowy outlines of men finished unloading the boat and filling the wagon before a tall man hopped up into the driver's seat beside the man already seated there, and they took off. A handful of remaining men, John Caney among them, dragged the boat up onto the sand before following the wagon up the rise.

A deep, incoherent voice broke through the quiet, and Pippa turned sharply toward Mr. Ainsworth to find him stirring. She jumped to her feet, backing away.

The wagon had yet to reach the top of the rise, and the men were still crossing the beach. Pippa wiped the sand from her cloak, searching the darkness for the figure which best resembled William, but it was too difficult to make out which man he was, despite the growing starlight.

Mr. Ainsworth continued to stir, mumbling now, though she still could not make out what he was saying. As relieved as she was that he appeared to be largely uninjured, his awareness was coming a few minutes too soon.

She needed to warn William.

CHAPTER 19

"*G*o! Run now!" Pippa yelled, heedless of who she alerted. She needed to warn William and his men to run for safety before Mr. Ainsworth located his senses and his weapon.

After her shout, Mr. Ainsworth ceased mumbling and pushed himself up into a seated position, his hand resting on the back of his head where she'd hit him. Urgency strung through the cold air, and the scuffle of men's feet running up the path sounded behind her, broken by the roaring of the waves crashing onto the sand.

"What happened?" Mr. Ainsworth asked, his voice groggy. He struggled to his feet.

Pippa picked up her skirts and ran before he could see her well enough to identify her.

"You there!" he called after her. "Who are you? What happened?"

Pippa ran faster. The men who'd done the illegal smuggling were gone, as far as she could tell. She made it halfway across the sand when someone grabbed her cloak from behind and yanked her back. She lost her footing and fell onto the sand, something hard cutting into her ribs like a piece of driftwood or a large rock. Mr. Ainsworth stood above her, panting, and rested his hands on his knees. He looked unsteady, and she rolled to the side and pushed to her feet.

Mr. Ainsworth lurched toward her but fell onto the sand, and she took the opportunity to run for the path again.

Someone took hold of her hand, and she attempted to yank it away, but couldn't get it free.

"It's me," William said harshly, pulling her toward the path his men had disappeared on. Warmth enveloped her in the safety of his voice. His grip was firm but gentle, nothing like the jarring attack from Mr. Ainsworth.

She looked over her shoulder to find Mr. Aisnworth on his feet again, and she tightened her hold on William's hand. "This way," she said quietly. She tugged him to the side, away from the main path. His men were gone, and the darkness consuming the side of the cliff extended down onto the sand beside it, covering them.

"Should we not attempt to get away?"

She pulled harder. "As long as he doesn't have his lantern, we'll be safe. Now cease talking and follow me. Is everyone else safe?"

"Yes."

She pinched her lips closed and tightened her hold on William's hand. He was without gloves, and the feel of his fingers wrapped around hers, albeit cold and clammy as they were, laid a blanket of encouragement over her.

"Where are we go—"

"Don't talk," Pippa said. They didn't know where Mr. Ainsworth had gone, or if the beach was clear yet. She led him toward the steep path that would deliver them directly in front of Camden Court. It was dangerous in the daylight—now it would be too unsafe to even attempt. But they could hide behind the rock at its entrance.

"Here," she whispered, releasing William's hand and pushing on his chest until he was flush against the rock. She tucked herself beside him and bent forward to peer around the rocky edge of the path. "I don't see him."

William put his hands on her shoulders and pulled her back into the safety of the inlet. "This was either brilliant—"

"Thank you."

"—or incredibly foolish."

Not what she'd wanted to hear. "In what way is this foolish? Your men are away safely, and you cannot be caught here."

"But we can be blocked in. No one is safe until the goods are stored, anyway. I should be with my men."

"Then go."

"I cannot leave you here."

"You needn't remain." She pressed herself further into the inlet, distancing herself from William enough so his hands fell from her shoulders. "Go. I can get myself home without being seen."

His low scoff reached her ears. "I am not leaving you."

"Perhaps I won't give you a choice." She turned away when his arms wrapped around her.

He pressed her back against the rock, bending his head until his lips were so close to her ear that she could feel his breath and tingles ran down her neck. "He's near."

Pippa's body stilled. She was less concerned with the presence of the law man and very much aware of the way her body reacted to William essentially holding her in an embrace. "And you need to hide me from him?" she whispered.

She could practically feel the smile stretching over his face. "I will not pretend that I am disliking this situation at all."

"Well, I am absolutely hating it," she quipped. She must turn to humor or the situation would grow far too serious. "Handsome gentlemen are constantly throwing themselves at me. It is really rather tedious."

"Quite."

"You don't believe me?"

His lips drew nearer to her ear, brushing along her skin as he spoke. "I heard nothing beyond you calling me handsome."

Drat. She should have phrased it differently. Words utterly escaped her, and Pippa considered for a moment how it would feel to turn her face just enough to meet her lips to his. She heard nothing besides the roaring waves and her own heartbeat thudding heavily in her ears.

"I'm certain you've been called handsome before. It really ought not to be such a shock."

"Perhaps I have. But never before by a woman I care about."

Cared about? Her? In what way had he even had ample opportunity to grow his regard for her? She felt anxious, nervous energy buzz about her body like an angry honeybee, and suddenly his arms around her and his head bent toward hers meant more than protecting her from Mr. Ainsworth.

She slid her hands up his chest and felt the moisture, his greatcoat dripping with water. How had she not noticed before how wet he was? Ah, the darkness. Of course.

William's chest expanded quickly under her fingers, and he lifted his head away from her ear. "I think he's gone."

"Or was he never really near?"

His low chuckle washed over her. "He was near. But I must thank you for the idea. Perhaps next time I find you alone on this beach I will likewise believe Mr. Ainsworth to be on our tails."

"I would not disapprove of that," Pippa said.

William's hand came up to cup her cheek, fumbling before it curved around her face, and his thumb brushed lightly over her cheekbone. "I can hardly see you, yet I can perfectly imagine your devious little smile."

Pippa longed to lean into his hand, to lift her face for his kiss, but she could not remove from her mind exactly how little he'd trusted her today. They had a ways to go yet before she would trust the man with her heart. To say nothing of the fact that Lily believed she had a claim on him as well. "If the way is clear, should you not go after your smuggled goods?"

William's thumb stilled. "I suppose you are correct. Though I will see you safely home, first."

"I know this beach and these paths better than anyone. Your father and your cousin might need you, William. You need to go."

He had no further argument for her, instead dropping his hold on her and stepping back. She cursed her own blasted tongue for stopping the man from kissing her. He took her by the hand and gently pulled her along behind him. They made their way toward the wide path up to the lane and Pippa pulled his arm when she heard footsteps above them. They waited a moment longer.

"Will?" a familiar voice called out quietly.

William's hand tightened on hers. "Who goes there?"

"'Tis only Samuel," he called.

Pippa leaned closer to William. "Samuel Caney?"

He grunted what she believed was a confirmation.

Pippa broke free of his grasp, but he stopped her. "You don't want to be seen."

"John Caney already saw me—"

"Yes, but not alone with a gentleman in the dark."

"You cannot honestly think my reputation would suffer for this."

"Why are you alone with a man in the dark on a secluded beach, Pippa? Why did you arrive at the cove at all in the middle of the night? Can you answer these things with good reasons?"

She couldn't. She'd awoken from the storm and seen the ship's light and followed the impulse to go to the beach. None of which were good reasons.

"William? You coming?" Samuel called.

"Yes, be up soon." William lowered his voice. "Let me go ahead. Wait for us to leave."

"So it is safe for you to leave me *now?*" she challenged.

He let out a frustrated breath. "Has anyone ever told you how difficult you are, Pip?"

"Yes."

He chuckled. "I must go. Be *safe.*" He leaned down and pressed a kiss to her cheekbone before turning and jogging—dangerously, in Pippa's opinion—to the top of the lane. She heard his low voice quietly speak and disappear as he and Samuel made their way in the direction of Ravenwood Cottage.

Her body grew warm, a silly smile stretching over her lips as she picked her way quietly back to her house. She wasn't sure if what she was feeling was merely attraction or the faint beginning of deeper feelings, planted and nurtured and starting to sprout like a seedling in new soil.

Whatever they were, William certainly returned them, and the idea made her belly warm. She made it to her front door and slipped inside before turning and locking the door behind her.

William followed the now-familiar lane toward his cottage, absently questioning Samuel on the details of what had happened after they separated at the beach, but his mind was not attending. His thoughts were locked on the moment when he'd had his arms around Pippa and his mouth so close to hers. He'd initially thought that covering her body with his had been a necessity. Despite the darkness, her scarlet cloak could have been easier to discern and given them away when Ainsworth passed by. William had done his best to protect them from being found by covering her with his own black-clad body.

But the moment he'd touched her, he'd known his mistake. Ainsworth's danger hadn't lasted long, and William had known the moment the revenue man had retreated, but he hadn't been able to back away from Pippa. He'd wanted to kiss her, had hoped she'd wanted to kiss him as well. He'd merely been waiting for her to grant her permission in some way.

But it hadn't come. Perhaps he shouldn't have kissed her cheek before leaving her, but he was struggling with his need for her, and it had been a moment of weakness. Seeing her on that beach with a knocked-out exciseman had been a shock, but it likely shouldn't have been. She seemed to be the sort of lady who often found herself in just these sorts of scrapes.

They rounded the corner and reached Ravenwood Cottage, but it was dark and quiet, the empty stillness reaching him with surety.

"Where is everyone?"

Samuel grimaced. "Likely gone on to the church, I suppose."

"Why?" William faced the lad. He was wet, tired, and wanted nothing more than to strip his soaked clothing from his clammy skin and slide into the sorry excuse for a bed waiting for him upstairs. "Why have they gone to the church, Samuel?"

"There's an old hideaway in the back of the chapel. Your father planned to use it if the revenue man found us, to keep the goods off your property."

William wanted to curse. Instead, he clapped Samuel on the back and shook his head. "Do you know how to reach the church in the dark? A back way, perhaps?"

Samuel nodded, just as eager to prove himself as William had hoped. "Just this way."

William gestured to the path before him and indicated that Samuel lead the way. He had a feeling he would not be falling into bed until just before the sun decided to awaken. Puffing a long breath through his nose, he followed the lad into the dark.

CHAPTER 20

*T*he congregation was quiet and stagnant the following day in church, as though everyone knew of the activity which had taken place among its parishioners the evening before and were focused on keeping the secret tightly sealed behind motionless lips. Mr. Ainsworth sat near the back. Pippa had nearly sunk to the floor when she saw him enter the building but forced herself to remain as though nothing were amiss. If he'd not recognized her last night as the woman he'd spoken to outside the Burkes' home, she did not intend to notify him of that detail.

Her best course of action was to pretend as though nothing were wrong and she had decidedly *not* whacked this stranger over the head with a dried branch of driftwood just a few hours before.

Mr. Robinson stood at his pulpit and preached to a crowd who did not seem to be paying him the least heed. Pippa tried to focus on the vicar and his words, but her attention was drawn continually to the man in a tall, black hat sitting in the row just behind her, all the way on the end of the pew. If she turned to speak to Elinor, she could see him in her peripheral vision. But she did not need to see William to feel his attention prickling her skin or recall the nearness of his lips when they'd hidden in the cove.

Pippa had very nearly leaned forward and kissed William last night. She sat on the hard pew and tried to recall what had stopped her. She really should have done it, if only to know what it felt like.

When the sermon came to an end, the congregation rose and meandered out to the churchyard in a slow progression like a herd of lazy cows. Pippa's eagerness made the crawl all the more painful. She followed James out of the pew to make their way toward the door just behind Mabel, the rest of their family following.

William stood from his seat, his hands resting casually before him, holding his hat. He watched her walk past him closely, and Pippa forced her eyes to remain anywhere *but* William's face for fear that if she were to meet his eyes, she would not be able to move another step. The question had plagued her mind over and over again since leaving him on the beach the evening before, and she was eager to ask it of him, to discover what William felt for her.

Mabel laughed at something just behind her, but Pippa kept her gaze on the floor. They passed into the walkway, and Pippa's eyes finally lifted just in time to land on Mr. Ainsworth. She froze.

He peered at her through a pair of confused, gray eyes. Was he connecting that she was the woman with the nearly-lethal driftwood from the beach the evening before? She delivered a quick smile to put him from that line of thought. Surely a woman who knocked him over the head would not be able to smile at him in a church the following morning.

Well, she had done just that a moment ago, but surely Mr. Ainsworth would not believe her *capable* of such.

Pippa had ascertained that the man looked whole and well,

thus appeasing some of her concern, and now she needed to flee. She would make it her business to avoid William in the churchyard. Mr. Ainsworth would not make the connection between them if she did not lead him to it.

Dropping her gaze to the floor once more, Pippa followed James's hurried steps toward the back door where Mr. Robinson stood to greet all his parishioners.

Her muffled steps slid over the stone floor, and she paused when she noticed a stone in the far back corner of the church, just beyond Mr. Ainsworth's feet, that sat a bit ajar, as though someone had pried it loose and hadn't replaced it properly. That was odd.

"Pip, have you inquired with the Burkes about dinner this evening?" Mabel asked, leaning forward and lowering her voice.

Pippa looked over her shoulder into her sister's familiar dark navy eyes. "I haven't had the opportunity yet. Did you not send round a note?"

Mabel's lips pressed together. "I will go find Edith and speak with her now. I should have written a note, but I didn't want to give them ample time to devise their excuse."

Suppressing her smile, Pippa stepped past the vicar and into the churchyard, moving to the side to allow Mabel to pass. The sun was covered, blanketed by gray clouds that filled the sky in every direction. A chill swept over her body, and she wrapped her arms around her waist, pulling her spencer jacket tightly over her shoulders.

"You are avoiding me," William's deep voice said just behind her.

Pippa worked to maintain a neutral expression despite the jumping in her heart. "I did not think it wise to bring attention to our relationship."

"We have a relationship then?"

She could hear the smile in his voice.

"Yes. I should like to think that you are my friend. Are you not?"

He stepped around to face her, his chin jutting forward as he looked up at the gray clouds and feigned rumination. "Friends," he said, as though tasting the word and determining his opinion on the flavor. "I'm not quite sure that is an appropriate label for what we are."

"Why is that?"

The Hoskins passed near them, and they both quieted and smiled at the couple, waiting until they were not within listening range before continuing. "Well, Roger is my friend, and I do not typically find myself gazing at his lips when he speaks."

Heat bled up Pippa's cheeks, and her gaze sought Roger of its own accord. He stood on the other side of the churchyard speaking to Mr. Burke and Lily, Mac just beside her.

"Is that all?" she asked, unable to help herself. It was a dangerous game she was playing, but that only made it all the more fun.

"I also don't imagine the feel of Roger's hand holding mine."

"Really? Why not?"

William's steady gaze beat down on her, the sunshine that was missing from this chilly afternoon. "I think he would find it odd."

A loud laugh rolled out of Pippa's chest, and she shook her head, unable to dampen the grin splitting her cheeks. "You are ridiculous."

William's grin mirrored her own. "Perhaps."

He failed to argue further, and she was equal parts grateful and perturbed when Mabel approached and put an end to their private conversation. Pippa had meant to ask about Ainsworth and whether or not William had been able to adequately hide everything he needed to, but his charm had distracted her.

"I do not see your father here today," Mabel said. "Is he planning to join us for dinner this evening?"

William's playful ease slipped away immediately, replaced with a tight smile. "He was not feeling quite the thing this morning, and he chose to remain home and rest today in hopes of healing quickly. He was very sorry to miss church, of course. He'll be even sorrier to miss dinner, Mrs. MacKenzie."

"Oh, dear. I do hope it is nothing too awful."

"A trifle, really," William explained. "I believe he overdid himself yesterday."

She seemed to take this well and nodded. "Come, Pip. We should be heading home."

"I would like to walk today."

Mabel looked as though she meant to argue. "It looks like rain. After the storm last night, the ground is—"

"I would be happy to escort Miss Sheffield home if that would put you at ease, Mrs. MacKenzie."

Pippa glanced up sharply. A public escort like that was nothing short of an announcement in Collacott. And until she was able to have a private, honest conversation with Lily, she could do nothing of the sort.

"I suppose I ought to return with you, Mabel. We wouldn't want to keep our dinner guests waiting." She shot William a smile, but his expression was confused, and she didn't blame him. He may have been clear about his feelings for her, but until she was certain of where Lily stood, there would be no future tête-à-têtes.

She slid her hands together and held them in front of her, dipping a soft curtsy to William before following Mabel toward Mac and the children. William's gaze was heavy on her back, and she felt the strength of it skitter over her skin. She hazarded a glance over her shoulder and caught his smirk. His dark eyebrow ticked up, and Pippa immediately tore her attention away from him, but not before the damage was done and her heart had effectively vaulted in her chest.

William was a fool if he did not comprehend exactly how

much Pippa was drawn to him. It frightened her how often she thought of him. She approached Lily, and guilt crawled up her limbs and wrapped around her like ivy on a stone wall. She needed to speak to her friend, and soon.

"We won't be joining you this evening," Lily said, pushing her bottom lip out in a slight pout. "Mother already set dinner to simmer before we left for church. She won't waste it."

Pippa knew a moment's temptation to argue that they could push the meal Mrs. Burke prepared until tomorrow's dinner, but she bit her tongue.

"You will be missed." Pippa lowered her voice and leaned in. "Have there been any more developments regarding a certain gentleman?"

Lily looked sharply toward where William and Roger were mounting their horses. "Not since yesterday, no. And you oughtn't speak of it so publicly. Someone could overhear."

Unease tightened Pippa's stomach. "If you are so certain of your feelings, why must you keep the liaison a secret?"

Lily flattened her lips. "I cannot very well announce my feelings until he's admitted to returning them, can I?"

Oh, dear. It was just as Pippa had expected. Lily's feelings were not returned if William spoke true, and Pippa did believe him. Worse, William had inferred he held a regard for Pippa, and the only reason Lily entertained the idea of a relationship with the man was because of Pippa's encouragement.

She looked into Lily's blue eyes, and bile clawed up her throat. What a mess she'd created. Taking Lily by the hand, she dragged her away from the groups of people converging and chatting in the churchyard until they were clear of all listening ears. She cared about Lily far too much to allow this to go any further.

But if William was an innocent man in all this, why had he not cleared up the misunderstanding with Lily already? Why did he allow it to continue? Pippa found him beyond the crowd sitting atop his horse, and he was watching her closely. Or was he watching Lily? She had not known the man long enough to ascertain whether he was playing a game with her heart, or if Lily was merely confused.

"I believe we have fallen for the same man." Pippa swallowed. "And I worry that he has allowed both of us to believe that he holds us in similar regard."

Lily's large, blue eyes widened, and she tipped her chin down. "What do you mean?"

"You've not received any sort of confirmation from Mr. Blakemore himself that he has any special regard for you, correct?"

"Correct."

"Yet he's given you ample reason to assume that that is the case."

Lily's cheeks pinked, and the rock settled in the pit of Pippa's stomach nestled further, weighing heavily. What had William done to elicit that blush in Lily? "Indeed."

Pippa thought of William's soft embraces, of the way he held her in the dark, his lips hovering near her ear, and she swallowed hard. "He's given me similar cause."

A stricken look passed over Lily's face. "I cannot believe it of him."

"Neither can I." And it was the truth. Pippa considered how genuine William's words felt, how deeply they'd resonated within her. Only a cunning man could lead two women to believe he was falling in love with both of them at the same time—and a man capable of such deceit would surely lie about it. When Pippa had asked him about Lily and he'd denied flirting with her, she'd believed him.

She scoffed at her own naiveté. "He is truly a wolf, is he not? He's fooled us both." Pippa should have worn her scarlet cloak today, for it was a fitting representation of how deeply she had been duped. "He is coming to dine at Camden Court tonight. What shall I say?"

"You could accidentally pour your glass of wine over his waistcoat," Lily offered. "Are you having fish? You ought to spill your dinner on his lap."

"I suppose I could concoct something," Pippa said. She tried to smile but her heart wasn't in the jest. She should have felt more justified in Lily's plot of revenge, but instead, her chest surged in pain. How could she have allowed herself to believe William's flirtations? She knew from the beginning that he'd resembled the wolf in *The Little Red Riding Hood*, yet she'd allowed her heart to be swindled, allowed him to take root in her soul.

And even worse, she'd flirted back.

Pippa allowed Lily to pull her in for a hug, righteous indignation undoubtedly covering the hurt Lily too must have felt.

"Will you cook for them tomorrow?" Pippa asked.

Lily lifted her shoulder. "Yes. What choice do I have? I may drop some extra salt in the stew, though."

Pippa bade her farewell and went to climb into the wagon behind Mabel. She watched the empty lane as they passed the turnoff toward Ravenwood Cottage, and her mind churned. She would see him again in a few short hours, and she didn't know how she was going to react to being in his presence again.

But one thing was for certain: she would not allow him to swindle her any further.

As they continued on toward their house, frustration bubbled and simmered in Pippa's chest like a pot of stew above a fire until she could no longer sit still. She needed to run, to climb . . . anything but sit like a docile lamb. She needed to get out of this wagon.

The cove came into view, and Pippa's gaze was drawn to the rock formation protruding near the peak in the cove.

"Wait," Pippa called.

Mac glanced at her over his shoulder, and she put her hand up to stop him. "Let me out here."

"Are you mad, Pip?" Mabel said, confusion clouding her brow. "We have guests coming. You cannot go down to the beach now."

"I won't be long," Pippa said, already making her way toward the edge of the wagon as Mac slowed the horse. She gripped the rough edges of the wagon and jumped down, her feet sinking into the marshy, water-laden ground.

"I really don't think you—"

"I'll be quick, I promise," Pippa called. "I'll be home before the guests arrive."

She didn't wait to see if Mabel believed her or give ample time for her niece and nephew to beg to accompany her. She couldn't have children along for what she wanted to do.

No, she needed to be alone. She was going to climb the rock.

CHAPTER 21

*P*ippa made it to the base of the enormous rock formation jutting out of the rock pools at the edge of the cove. She looked up and knew a moment's hesitation. The sheer enormity of the rock was much larger when standing at its base than it appeared from the beach. She swallowed her reserve and stepped over the wet sand from the receded tide. She needed to push herself as much as she was able, to get her heart thudding in a way that William could not claim ownership of.

She was angry with him, but more at herself for falling victim to his flirtatious ways. The cad.

Wedging her foot into a low groove, Pippa pulled herself up and began to climb. It was not overly steep, and the climb would have been fairly simple even for the children, but her skirt whipping in the wind did make it a little more complicated than she had hoped. She kept to the side that pressed nearly against the sheer cliffside, focusing her attention on locating proper footholds. Pippa might break convention with her climbing habits, but she was not reckless.

She crested the peak she was on and looked over her

shoulder at the beautiful view of the waves crashing against the rocks and the tips of Camden Court on the other side of the cove's curve. The thudding of her heart pulsed in her ears. Black birds swooped over the sky and landed on a rock further out to sea. She wanted to climb higher, but she'd promised Mabel she'd return before their guests arrived, and that didn't leave her much time.

Breathing in the salty air, Pippa felt refreshed. Her heart pounded, her chest heaved, and her muscles ached softly from the exertion. She *felt*, and it had nothing to do with William. It was rejuvenating.

She had allowed herself to fall victim to a handsome man and his cunning tongue, but she would not give him more of herself. It was a blessed thing she had not allowed him to kiss her, for that would only have made the hurt more acute.

Pippa turned to find the best pathway to descend, saving the higher peak for another day and a skirt which lent itself better to climbing. A narrow, dark inlet caught her eye up against the side of the cliff. It looked to be a small cave set up the cliffside at least the height of two fully grown men standing feet to head. Pippa scrambled closer. An array of twigs and dried grass poked from the edge. A bird had nested within the small cave, but by the look of the broken shells and bits of twigs, they were long gone.

She reached from her perch to the cliffside and moved the nest over. She couldn't see how far back the little cave reached, but she imagined it had been a bird refuge for many years, tucked away as it was into the side of the cliff and not easily accessible.

Pippa had never noticed it herself, and she'd been coming to this beach for more than half her life. Birds often flew around up here, but they perched on the rock she was currently standing upon and she'd never looked to the shadowed cliffside and expected more.

After one final lungful of salty air, Pippa climbed down from the rock until her feet were securely on the wet rock pools at its base. She stepped back and took in the majestic rock. She had only made it just over halfway up, but that was high enough for today. She searched for the bird's refuge and found it easily, the space darker than the rest of the cliffside.

Shadows dripped down the rocky side where the cliff shape undulated and shifted, but she could easily pinpoint the cave's location. It was so plain to see now that she knew where it was. Perhaps she hadn't noticed it before because she hadn't known where to look.

Pippa watched the birds fly over the rock for a few minutes more, but none of them went near the cave, reinforcing her belief that the bird who'd been using it was now gone. Gathering herself, she turned back for her house.

It was time to have dinner with a wolf.

William approached the tree-lined drive to Camden Court with anticipation to see Pippa, but worry lodged in his gut and refused to vacate. Worry that they wouldn't be able to clear the church of their products in time, that Ainsworth would descend at any moment and arrest Roger for the shooting in Dorset, that William would never be free of the duty he felt to aid his father and brother.

Roger walked at his side, a smug smile lifting his lips. "Why so glum, Will?"

Despite his eagerness to see Pippa again, Will could not erase the memory of Ainsworth's calm expression from earlier that day. *Too* calm. The man's confidence filled William with trepidation. Ainsworth should have been upset to have come so close to catching William and his men, and having them slip through his fingers.

Because the only explanation William could reasonably understand was that Ainsworth planned to exact his revenge by putting all of them in gaol, and not settling for just Roger. Otherwise, he could have already moved on Roger's arrest, could he not?

William looked at his friend in mild confusion. "Are you not worried at all? You saw Ainsworth's face at the church today. He wasn't troubled in the least."

Roger's smile slipped. Ah, so he was concerned, even if he tried to hide it. It was a little comforting to know he didn't believe himself invincible. "The man doesn't have enough evidence to arrest me, or he would have done so by now."

"That is one theory. Perhaps his purpose in coming here is to gather enough evidence to arrest you. To arrest us all." William shook his head. "We're being foolish by pretending otherwise."

Roger paused on the walkway and grabbed William's arm. His angular face grew shadowed and serious. "I am not unaware of the danger here, Will. I am merely not allowing it to show so readily. You needn't remind me how my neck was on the line. I felt it keenly."

"Was?"

"Yes, *was*. If Ainsworth had just cause to arrest me, he would have done it the moment he located us. But the night was so dark when *it* happened, and I'm fairly certain—*no*, I'm positive he did not see who shot the gun."

William shrugged his arm free. Roger made a valid observation. "That's an interesting point. I couldn't understand why Ainsworth hadn't yet made his move, but perhaps you're correct. Maybe the darkness protected you, if only just." And in doing so, made all of them a target. If Ainsworth did not know who to blame, would he indeed blame them all? Father must have made their guilt obvious by forcing them to flee. No one else left Dorset except the three of them.

Father must not have considered that to begin with or he

wouldn't have believed that bringing Roger to Collacott would protect him. Though in his own words, they'd never been truly hiding.

They approached the front door of Camden Court and were let inside by a servant who took their discarded coats and hats. Voices came from the drawing room, filtering into the hall and wrapping about William like a warm, comforting blanket. He was eager to join the Mackenzie family, and even more excited to see Pippa. He crossed into the room just after Roger and met with Mac's tall form near the door. They exchanged pleasantries and lamented the water-bogged earth due to the previous night's storm, but William's attention was repeatedly drawn back to Pippa's straight back, facing him from the far window. She bounced Liam on her hip and hadn't moved from her position watching out the window since he'd arrived.

Had she been watching him approach the house? Surely she was not ignorant of his presence in the room.

And yet, she still would not turn and face him.

Mrs. Mackenzie ushered them into the seating area beside the fire. "I've instructed my cook to prepare a basket for your father. Is he feeling any better?"

William recalled the way he'd left Father at the door, the man walking toward the church while he and Roger left for Camden Court. He was well enough if he could check on their hidden stores in the church.

Roger rescued him from being forced to devise a lie. "He'll be grateful for whatever you send, ma'am."

Mrs. Mackenzie smiled kindly. "I hope you don't mind that we dine rather informally here. I've not been one to concern myself too greatly with even numbers."

William liked her for it. He'd watched his mother try to fit in with the gentry in Dorset and anxiously analyze herself. Everything fell under scrutiny from what she wore to what she served to how she spoke. Father wanted acceptance, and Mother wanted to make Father happy. Perhaps that was part of why William had felt so drawn to Pippa from the beginning—she was a woman who knew her own mind.

"We don't mind in the least," William said to put Mrs. Mackenzie at ease.

Mrs. Mackenzie crossed to the window and took Liam from Pippa's arms, saying something softly to her sister. Pippa's head turned and he got a glimpse of her face for the first time since arriving, and she did not look pleased. She appeared to be arguing with her sister as her arms were folded across her chest, the position of a defensive woman.

Oh, no. What happened? She'd been perfectly amiable in the churchyard earlier. She crossed the room behind her sister, and all the while avoided meeting William's gaze. Mrs. Mackenzie handed her babe off to a stout maid, who also ushered the other children from the room.

Mac slid his arm around his wife's waist. "Shall we head in to dinner?"

A loud knock at the front door drew the attention from everyone in the room. Pippa turned and looked out the window again, her brow puzzled. The moment it cleared, she looked to William sharply, and he was arrested by the magnitude of her direct gaze. He wanted to get her alone so he could ask what was bothering her.

Pippa dragged her gaze toward her brother-in-law. "It's Mr. Ainsworth."

Mac looked confused. "Mae, did you invite him to dine with us?"

"No, though I suppose it wouldn't be impossible to set another place. Shall I go speak to Cook?"

Mac shot an apologetic look at William and Roger. "That might be wise. Let us wait and see what he is here for, first."

The same servant who'd let William in earlier opened the drawing room door and presented Ainsworth.

"Forgive my intrusion," Ainsworth said, his greasy smile the very opposite of contrite. "I did not intend to interrupt your evening."

"Nonsense," Mrs. Mackenzie said politely. "When I mentioned at church today that you are welcome to come by any time, I meant it."

"We are about to sit to dinner," Mac said. "Would you care to join us?"

"Oh, I could never impose. There is a perfectly adequate meal awaiting me at the White Swan Inn, I'm sure." He did not move as though he meant to leave, however, and after a few moments, Mrs. Mackenzie stepped forward, her hands clasped softly before her.

"I insist you stay and join us," she said. "If you would like to sit, Mr. Ainsworth, I must go attend to a few things, but I will return shortly."

She was undoubtedly going to tell her servants to prepare an additional setting at the table.

Mac indicated a seat on the sofa and Ainsworth took it, smugly passing William and Roger as though he had been the invited guest and they the interlopers. "You mentioned earlier that you are here on business, correct?" Mac asked.

"Indeed." Ainsworth looked at William and then Roger. "I have come to settle a debt."

"Oh, how unpleasant," Pippa said. She crossed the room and took the seat beside Mac. "I would think that quite odious."

"It must needs be done. Though the task is difficult, I am a patient man."

A patient man. He had a plan, then. William did his best to look at ease, to hide the turmoil this fed into his body.

"Will you remain in Collacott for long, then?" Mac asked.

"As long as I need to," Ainsworth said with a rodent-like smile. His angular chin and nose were reminiscent of a rat, and

William wanted to swipe the satisfied look from his face. The man was the worst sort of rudeness.

Mrs. Mackenzie returned and indicated they could move into the dining room. Pippa fell back to the last, and William attempted to walk beside her, but she angled her face away from him.

"Pippa—"

She startled him with a swift glare, and his words died on his tongue. Something had most definitely occurred to anger her. Her beautiful eyes could spit fire.

They took their seats around the table, and William found himself sitting directly across from Pippa, who was sandwiched between Roger and Ainsworth.

Mrs. Mackenzie sat to William's right, and she shot him a patient smile. "Tell me, Mr. Blakemore, have you missed Dorset a great deal?"

"I haven't," he said and found that his answer was truthful. He hadn't once wished to be back in his old house—though he had on multiple occasions wished his old bed had been brought with them to Devon. His first order of business when he found a spare moment would be to go into town and order new beds and mattresses. They had certainly been long enough without them. "I've enjoyed Collacott quite a lot."

"The people here truly are humble and kind."

"I've experienced that, and I must agree. I found myself wondering how my father ever convinced my mother to leave it."

Mrs. Mackenzie took a bite and chewed it slowly. "Sometimes we have little choice in where we settle to raise our children. I did not intend to live here in Camden Court, but I am glad this is the direction my life took me."

"Where would you have preferred to be?"

"Here, now that I know it. My entire life was spent in Graton though, and I never thought I would be capable of leaving. My friends are all there, and my connections to my mother are there. But I've made a home here, and I'm certain now I could never leave Collacott."

William's fork stalled just before reaching his mouth. "I suppose we make our home wherever our family is."

"Indeed," Mrs. Mackenzie agreed. She lifted her goblet and took a sip of wine before cutting into her potatoes.

The conversation taking place on the other side of the table caught William's ear and he stilled, listening carefully to what Ainsworth was saying. "When I was in the taproom the other night, I heard reports of smuggling activity on these shores. Surely that does not affect you here, Mr. Mackenzie? Your home is so close to the cove."

Mac's eyebrows drew together. "Smuggling in our cove? You must be mistaken."

Mrs. Mackenzie's utensils stilled above her plate, her arms frozen. A look passed between her and Pippa, and William wanted to know what it meant. Had Pippa told her sister about her adventure in the middle of the night?

"I would not expect a navy man such as yourself to participate in such illegal activity," Mr. Ainsworth said, affecting nonchalance. "But I did wonder if you've seen it occurring. Heard whispers on late nights passing by your windows."

"I assure you, Mr. Ainsworth, I've heard no such whispers. I wouldn't be partial to smuggled goods passing my windows, either."

"No, of course not," Ainsworth said. He swiveled a look in William's direction, and all William could do was stare back, hard. He wished it had been him and not Pippa who had hit this man over the head, for no other reason than the satisfaction it would give him.

"Enough talk of such things at dinner, please," Mrs. Mackenzie said with a light smile. The woman was an adept hostess. She steered the conversation onto the neutral topic of the fish trade and inquired about the fare available at the inn. By the time they were through with dinner, William was sore from tensing his muscles and forcing himself to remain calm.

It was evident that Ainsworth was playing a game with them, and William intended to end it. Tonight.

CHAPTER 22

*M*ac had been quiet since the conversation at dinner had steered toward smuggling, and Pippa was concerned about what this could mean for the Blakemores. The men remained in the dining room after the meal's conclusion while Pippa followed Mabel into the foyer.

"That man is impertinent," Mabel said softly, leaning close to Pippa as she spoke. "Sitting to dine with us like that? He ought to have refused. It would have been the polite thing to do."

"He is clearly not concerned with politeness."

Mabel nodded absently. "Do you know what debt he has come to collect?"

Pippa shook her head. "I know nothing of him short of what he told me when I met him in town. He's a law man."

"A law man who has come to collect? Something is not adding up." She glanced over her shoulder toward the closed door of the dining room. "Do you think the Blakemore men have been smuggling in the cove like Mr. Ainsworth seems to believe? I'm certain he was targeting them with that comment."

Pippa held her breath. If she was going to reveal her late-night antics to Mabel, now was a good opportunity. But if she did, would Mae revoke the freedoms she willingly gave Pippa now and keep her locked in her room? It was better not to risk it.

"Would it be so awful if they were?" Pippa asked instead.

Mabel seemed to think this over. "People in town don't seem too bothered by it. I believe it goes against Mac's morals, but I know people have been getting away with it for years, and it does provide affordable goods to those who need it."

"Or wine to our father."

Mabel smiled faintly, but her mind was elsewhere.

"You do not seem convicted in your opinions," Pippa pressed.

"Perhaps because I cannot make up my mind. I can see both sides to this situation."

"As can I," Pippa said. She would not admit to her sister how very much embroiled she was in the whole of it. She had a feeling Mac would never approve, and she did not like the idea of making him think less of her. She respected him far too much.

And to think, when she first believed William to be in trouble, she had offered to fetch Mac and his reputation to assist. As if Mac would help in a smuggling endeavor. The thought was humorous now, and a small smile tugged at her lips.

"Did you think of Gram's warning during dinner?" Mabel asked, holding the door open to the drawing room before closing it behind them.

"Yes," Pippa admitted. But she'd also thought of the moment when she'd hit Mr. Ainsworth over the head and how that had implicated her in the smuggling. She had a feeling Mabel would be generally less intrigued and far more angry if Pippa were to admit that now, however.

"And do you still hold it against the men? After spending some time with them, I wonder if perhaps you've been a bit hasty in your dismissal of the Blakemores."

Pippa looked sharply at her sister. "I did not hold it against them . . . well, I suppose I did initially. I'm not sure how I feel any longer. Gram does not seem bothered by it."

"Gram came from a different era, Pip. They saw things much differently back then than we do now."

"Does a change in perspective make the actions themselves any different? Our perspectives shift, but have they shifted in the proper way, or are we now in the wrong?"

Mabel lowered herself onto the sofa, her lips flat and eyebrows bunched. "I'm not sure. I suppose we would think our way to be correct because it is how we were raised to think. Gram would undoubtedly think her way correct. Who's to say which is better?" She jutted her chin out just a little. "I would like to think that with time comes wisdom, but I wonder if there is truth in both ways of thought. We must discern where the truth lies."

"So you mean to say that there is no clear answer."

Mabel grinned. "There is certainly no clear answer. I suppose this comes down to trusting ourselves and our own morals. We are good people, Pip. That counts for something, and it means we can listen to the whispers in our hearts."

But the whisper in Pippa's heart was hardly a whisper any longer. It nearly shouted William's name, and the man had proven to be less than savory.

Or *had* he proven it yet? He deserved an opportunity to defend himself, surely. Though she'd attempted to give him that before, and he'd acted as though he had no inclination why Lily would even imagine a liaison between them.

Pippa didn't know who to trust, and it made her heart ache wearily.

The drawing room door opened, and the men stepped inside. William's cool blue gaze sought hers, and Pippa had difficulty looking away. Mabel moved beside her, and it shook her from her William-induced trance. She looked away and found Mr.

Ainsworth watching her with mild interest before he looked to William.

Oh, drat. They'd shared a look, and Ainsworth had noticed. This could not be good.

Mrs. Mackenzie rose and ushered the men to take their seats. William watched Pippa avoid him, looking everywhere but at his face, it seemed. He'd thought they had just shared a moment when he came into the room, but apparently she wanted to believe differently. He needed to get her alone and ask what had happened to alter her opinion of him.

But how was he to accomplish that?

"Shall we retrieve the cards?" Mac asked, following the men to the seating area. "Does anyone enjoy playing?"

Roger lit up. "I've been known to dabble."

William swallowed a scoff. Yes, *dabble*. If that meant losing hundreds at the faro tables on a regular basis. At least coming to Devon had been good for Roger's pocketbook.

"Shall we play a round of whist?" Mabel looked about the room as if counting the guests. "Or speculation?"

"I can sit out and watch," William said. Perhaps if Pippa did the same, they would have the opportunity to speak.

She looked up and held his gaze. "I would love to play whist."

"Wonderful. Would you like to partner me?" Roger asked.

Pippa turned her brilliant smile on him. "I would like that very much."

Cards were sent for, and the table put together. Mac opted to sit out and moved closer to William's chair. He leaned back and stretched his legs out before him. "Has your father enjoyed returning to his old house?"

No. He complained of the beds, the chill in the air, and the lack of comforts more than Roger. "He has grown accustomed to a different quality of life in Dorset, so I think the cottage has been uncomfortable for him."

Mac's confused brow asked the question that he was too polite to voice. *If he was more comfortable in Dorset, why has he moved back to Collacott?*

William shifted in his seat. He really needed to cease fidgeting or he would give himself away for the fraud he was. "He has really enjoyed seeing old friends and being in the place where he spent his youth. I wondered if it would be difficult for him to return to the place where he married my mother, but he seems to be glad of the good memories."

"Does your mother still have family here?"

"No, she never did. She was orphaned young and worked as a maid in a house in Melbury." William spoke the truth with no shame. He was not afraid of where he'd come from. His father had made good money as a smuggler and clawed them out of a life of labor and drudgery. A few good investments later, and the Blakemores never needed to work again.

They continued to smuggle for other reasons. Or so Father said. William was struggling to determine what those reasons could be.

Now he needed to turn the conversation back toward Mac. "Have you missed the navy?"

"I miss the ocean sometimes, and the men. But that is part of the reason we chose this house so close to the sea. It has kept me near the water and the salty air I missed when I lived more inland."

"Perhaps that is what I need, as well," William said. "A house near the sea."

Mac looked surprised at this admission. "Have you been considering leaving the fishing industry?"

"I've enjoyed it, but I'm not yet sure if it is how I want to spend the rest of my days. I considered farming, but I wouldn't know the first thing about it."

"There are plenty nearby who would be happy to teach you. I have a great man who manages our fields. Mr. Winthrop. I can set up a meeting with him if you'd like to go over your options. He was at your fields that day."

"I recall meeting him."

"He's quite knowledgeable. Our land had been neglected when we moved here, and Winthrop knew exactly how to bring it back and make it fertile again. It takes skill to farm here. But you can learn."

"I would like to," William said, and his chest warmed with the reassurance that he meant those words. He imagined himself working his own land and the satisfaction that alone could bring. "If your man doesn't mind teaching, I should like to learn."

Mac's face split into an amused smile. "He enjoys sharing his knowledge. Trust me, you are the one doing him a favor."

William laughed, and a small glimmer of hope sprouted in his chest. A bright spot of light shining on his future and the possibilities waiting for him. He could make a home and a life here, and for the first time since coming to the damp cottage and uncomfortable straw mattress, he believed he just might be happy as well.

He watched the group on the other side of the room as they continued to play whist, and his gaze traced Pippa's profile. Would she be interested in the life he wanted to lay out for himself? Could he tempt her to Ravenwood Cottage and a humbler life than the one she was accustomed to? He had his savings; they would never be poor. But he didn't imagine he would ever call himself a wealthy man, either.

William would need to court her first, of course. The idea of which laid a pleasant warmth over his body.

Perhaps he should ask Mac's blessing to court her now while

he had a moment alone with the man. But, no. Pippa was unlike other women, and he could see that course of action being a deterrent to her. She was clearly unhappy with him at present.

She smiled at something Roger said, and it sent a spark through William's chest. He wanted that smile for himself.

"Do you know much about Mr. Ainsworth, there?" Mac asked, leaning close and lowering his voice. It dripped with distrust, which felt like a small victory for William.

"I don't trust him," William said quietly.

Mac looked as though he agreed, but didn't voice the opinion. "I do wish he would explain the nature of his business in a more exact way."

Neither of them said what they were both likely thinking, that it took a different character with little reserve to invite himself to dine with another's party.

The remainder of the evening was spent playing cards and watching the players, but William didn't mind. After Roger had played a few rounds, William rose from his seat. "Thank you for your hospitality, Mrs. Mackenzie."

Mrs. Mackenzie rose from the card table, the picture of poise, despite a slight limp. How had he not noticed it before? She was such a graceful creature, it undoubtedly went undetected by those who didn't know to look for it. "We've enjoyed your company this evening. I do hope your father will be able to join us next time."

"Certainly."

Mr. Ainsworth made no move to leave, and it occurred to William that perhaps the revenue man was simply waiting for them to leave so he could speak to Mac in privacy. The thought ran a cold wash of fear through his body, and he swallowed hard.

William didn't want Mac to think less of him, to learn of his disreputable past.

He made it to the door with Roger close behind him. Pippa

stood beside her sister and put enough distance between herself and William so he could not find a way to ask her to meet him later that evening. Of course, he wasn't sure if she'd even go if he had found the opportunity to ask, and he had no inkling as to why.

What had he done?

William walked across the gravel drive only a few moments later, Camden Court behind him and Roger at his side. He felt unfinished, uneven, without Pippa's smile to send him away, and the sensation settled uncomfortably in his gut.

He would find her tomorrow, and he would speak to her then.

CHAPTER 23

Four days had passed since the Blakemore men had come to dine, and Pippa had gone out of her way to stay clear of William. She did not trust herself around him yet. He was too romantic, too sweet, and she was too susceptible to his charm.

Gram sat in a chair near the fire in the drawing room and Pippa sat across from her, staring at the chessboard between them and deciding where she wanted to move. She had been losing horribly to Gram all morning, her mind so distracted and unable to focus on any sort of strategy.

Pippa slid her knight around a bishop, and Gram snorted.

"Are you trying to lose, Pip?"

"No." Well, not actively. Though she certainly wasn't trying to *win*, either.

Gram snorted again, then moved her bishop and stole Pippa's knight. "Check."

Drat. She hadn't seen that coming yet, but she could see now how she'd practically opened the pathway for Gram to take her king. What had she been thinking?

Oh, right. She hadn't been thinking at all.

"I think I need some fresh air."

Gram frowned, soft wrinkles creasing her forehead. "You spend too much time outside. It will ruin your complexion."

"It already has, Gram," Pippa said, leaning down to leave a kiss on her cheek. Gram pretended to swat her away, but the crotchety old woman's smile revealed her pleasure. She liked Pippa, and Pip knew it.

It was a moment's work to find her scarlet cloak and throw it over her shoulders, and she was outside shortly after, breathing in the salty air and tucking loose strands of hair back into the knot at the base of her neck. The wind increased, pulling at her skirts and wrapping them around her legs as she walked.

When she made it out of the tree-lined drive and onto the path, she pulled up short. A man stood on the edge of the cliff near the mouth of the path that led down to Camden Cove, his arms resting behind his back as he surveyed the beach. For a brief moment, she believed it to be William, but Mr. Ainsworth's lanky figure and downturned mouth could never pass as William for longer than a brief glance. He didn't have William's self-assured bearing or defined jawline.

Mr. Ainsworth turned and faced her, and she knew she could not sneak back into the comfort of the trees behind her. She stepped toward him and paused near the mouth of the beach path. "Good day, Mr. Ainsworth."

"It is a good day, indeed, Miss Sheffield. I have a good feeling about today." He bounced on the balls of his feet, and anxious energy sloughed from him in waves.

She tried to hide her surprise. "Have you been able to collect on your debt?"

Confusion lay over him briefly before he came to himself. "Not yet, but I have a feeling I shall by the end of the week. Things are lining up for me nicely, and now I simply must wait for . . . certain events to play themselves out."

Things were lining up for him? Could the events that would

play themselves out possibly be another smuggling endeavor? Surely it was too soon for William to do it again, particularly after almost being caught.

William needed to be warned.

"Well, if you'll excuse me," she said, gesturing to the path behind him. "I have an appointment with a friend I am late for."

"Must you walk far? I would be happy to accompany you."

"Not far at all." She stretched her smile further over her lips, but it didn't reach her eyes. "You recall Lily Burke? I believe we met for the first time just outside her door."

"Of course, but is her home not the other direction?"

"She works at Ravenwood Cottage."

Mr. Ainsworth blinked at her a few times. "And is that not the Blakemore cottage?"

"It is." She tried to smile again, but her cheeks were growing stiff and uncomfortable. "You are learning the people quite well for one so new. Good day, Mr. Ainsworth."

He lifted his hat to her, and she slipped around him, unwilling to invite the man to come along with her on this errand. Particularly when she hoped not to see Lily at all, and when Mr. Ainsworth was so suspicious. Had he seen her coming from the drive to Camden Court and connected that she was likely the person who'd hit him over the head on the beach? He'd grabbed at her cloak that night, the very cloak she wore now.

She must hope that the night had been too dark and his vision too faulty after awakening to recall those little details.

Swallowing hard, Pippa made it to the path that curved into Ravenwood Cottage and slipped through the woods. If she got lucky, perhaps she would find William outside, would be able to deliver her warning to him, and then could leave again swiftly.

There was no movement outside the cottage when she arrived, so Pippa picked her way quietly across the front garden toward the window that she knew would lead into the kitchen.

It was wise to speak to Lily, however briefly, to establish a purpose for being on Blakemore property.

Pippa stepped up to the kitchen window and peeked into the house. It was dim inside, and she had to squint to see. There was a figure on the far end of the room, and it looked—

Good heavens. Pippa pulled herself away from the window and flattened her back against the wall before she could be seen. She blinked the image from her mind, her breaths coming rapidly. Tears threatened, needling her nose as she squeezed her eyes shut.

Lily was wrapped in William's arms, kissing him so heavily that Pippa couldn't tell when one of them began and the other ended. Her stomach fell clear to the ground. She'd wanted so badly to be wrong about William, to believe the way he made her feel was real. But it was impossible to argue with the truth plainly present before her eyes.

A giggle floated from within the house and slapped her, and Pippa straightened. She wanted to get out of there fast, to not be discovered while learning the awful truth.

Motion in the trees alerted her to the presence of another person coming her way and she panicked, hurriedly wiping the tears from her cheeks and drying her hands down her gown. If Mr. Ainsworth had followed her, she would rather not have to explain her sudden burst of emotion.

Pippa looked up when the footsteps grew louder, and her eyes locked on William coming from the path in the woods.

But, how?

She rubbed at her eyes again, but he did not change. Pippa turned back for the window and peeked inside. She found Lily still wrapped in the arms of a man, but it wasn't William. It was Roger.

Roger Blakemore.

Now that she looked closer, she could see his blond hair shadowed in the dim kitchen, his face buried in Lily's neck. The pieces shifted and moved into place, and the truth smacked Pippa in the gut.

She and Lily had not been speaking about the same Mr. Blakemore. It was so clearly obvious now, Pippa felt keenly ridiculous for not having noticed before. Had either of them mentioned a Christian name during their conversations? Clearly, they'd both assumed "Mr. Blakemore" to be theirs. Pippa hardly spared Roger a thought in general, and she *never* thought of him as Mr. Blakemore, though she couldn't exactly say why that was.

It was the only explanation that made sense, especially given the current evidence in the Blakemores' kitchen. She hoped Lily had come to that same conclusion before this embrace occurred.

But more than that, this meant that her estimation of William's character had not been as off-kilter as she'd believed.

Cool relief flushed through Pippa's body even as she found his gaze pasted to her.

Pippa hurried across the lawn, meeting him at the mouth of the lane before he could speak and draw attention from the lovers inside. She would need to speak to Lily, but she didn't want to do so now.

William paused as she approached. She glanced both ways to be certain Mr. Ainsworth hadn't followed either of them, then took William by the hand and tugged him back down the path and into the woods.

"Do you have a spare minute?" she asked.

"Yes," he said, though he sounded confused. She didn't blame him. She hadn't tried to hide how deeply she'd been avoiding him. He must think her the strangest creature.

"Good."

Pippa pulled William away from the path and through the trees until she felt properly hidden. Surely even if Mr. Ainsworth had followed either of them, he would have stopped further back. She did not see a soul.

William's hand tightened around hers. She slipped her hand

free and stepped back. She needed space or her judgment would surely be clouded.

"Still upset with me, I see." He didn't look pleased, but he'd willingly followed her through the trees, so he couldn't be too angry with her.

"No, not upset. Not any longer."

His dark eyebrows lifted. "May I ask what I did to earn your ire in the first place? And furthermore, what did I do to dispel your frustration?"

"Nothing."

"You will not wound me by speaking the truth."

"No, William. I mean it. You did nothing. I was under the impression that . . . well, suffice it to say that I believed ill of you when you've done nothing wrong. I was mistaken. I did not trust you when you assured me that you did not give Lily cause to believe you loved her."

"Lily? Truly, I have not—"

"I know this now. She's currently wrapped in Roger's arms as we speak. Though perhaps I ought to have interfered and ended that before they were discovered by someone with a slippery tongue."

William opened his mouth to speak but said nothing.

Pippa folded her hands carefully before her. "Please do come out with it. What are you struggling to say right now?"

"I hadn't any idea that Lily and Roger were . . . well, I'm not certain Roger *loves* Lily either." William grimaced. "He merely loves women, and he has little loyalty to Collacott."

Anger pooled in Pippa's stomach, and she clenched her teeth. "Does your cousin not intend to remain here for long? He will merely break her heart and leave?"

"He's not my cousin, and no, he certainly does not intend to remain."

"Not your cousin?"

"No. He is my . . . colleague. I once would have called him

THE SMUGGLER OF CAMDEN COVE

my friend. Though recent circumstances have forced me to question why I respected him in the first place." William narrowed his eyes. "But Roger is not the reason you dragged me into the seclusion of the woods, is it?"

Seclusion. He was correct. They were utterly alone. Suddenly William appeared much taller, his shoulders broader and his icy blue eyes more striking.

Pippa fought the temptation to step away from him. She didn't feel threatened by William, just concerned about them being found alone together.

She cleared her throat. She'd come here with a purpose. "No, I came to warn you. I spoke with Mr. Ainsworth earlier today, and he implied that he was pleased because his debt was soon to be repaid."

William's body seemed to still, his intent eyes fastened on her.

Pippa continued. "He mentioned that things were falling into place and . . . well, I'm having trouble recalling his *exact* wording, but he did say he was hopeful it would be resolved soon. He seemed rather confident, like he had been tipped off about something, and he was watching the cove."

"Someone has told him, then." William rubbed his chin, his eyes focused in the distance.

"Told him what, exactly? Do you have another smuggling evening planned already?"

William chuckled, dropping his hand. "What exactly is a smuggling evening, Pippa?"

"You know," she said impatiently. "An evening where you smuggle things."

He laughed harder, his eyes resting softly on her.

"I do not know your jargon, William. You know perfectly well what I mean."

"I do, and I quite enjoy the way you phrased it."

She pursed her lips. "Why does that make me wish to never speak in front of you again?"

"Because you are contradictory to a fault. Something I find usually amusing and sometimes frustrating."

"And you, sir, are honest to a fault. Most of the time. So, what is it that Mr. Ainsworth believes he knows?"

His eyes lost some of the levity they'd previously possessed. "That a smuggling evening is coming, undoubtedly."

"When?"

"I cannot tell you that, Pip."

"Yes, you can. How can I help if I remain ignorant?"

His mouth firmed, and his voice hardened. "That is why you shall remain ignorant. I do not wish for your help. I would much prefer you stay safe at home."

"Well, I wouldn't."

"Clearly."

She put her fists on her hips. "William, I can help. Use me. You clearly don't have enough men."

"No."

Pippa huffed a frustrated breath. "Why do you underestimate me?"

William stared at her hard. He stepped forward and tugged one of her fists from her hips, then turned her hand over and opened her palm. He traced each of her fingers, leaving behind pools of heat where he touched her.

William looked at her hand while he spoke. "I am certain you are capable of leading the entire company of men. It is not that I underestimate you, Pippa, but that I value you too much. I . . . I lost my mother to a gunshot from a revenue man. She should not have gone with my father that night, but he needed someone to look out, and she was willing." He closed his eyes as if the pain from that memory had lashed him.

Pippa wanted to comfort him but didn't know how. She could understand his hesitance now. She took his hand in both of hers and ran her fingers along his palm in the same way he had done for her. He looked up, surprised, but then smiled. "I want to protect you, Pippa, and you know as well as I that Mac would have my head if he learned of my allowing you to participate in these clandestine activities. If nothing else, it's breaking the law."

That made her bristle. "Mac is not my father."

"No, but he loves you dearly, and in lieu of your father's presence, I'm certain I shall have to gain his blessing to court you."

Her heart skipped a beat. Court her? Good gracious, she would like that very much. Pippa's knees grew weak from the soft touch of her finger on his palm. She wanted to close her fingers around his and tug him close.

"Would you like that, Pippa?"

"For you to speak to Mac?"

"For me to court you."

"Oh, that." She was dizzy from his touch. Which way was up? The trees were so tall, they blocked the sky, and she felt cloaked in shadows and warmth. "I suppose it would be all right."

William laughed. "Your eagerness astounds me."

"If I am too eager, you may run away."

His free hand brushed a loose hair from her forehead. "That could not be further from the truth."

"So if I were to tell you I was devastated when I believed you might be playing me for a fool, you would not think less of me?"

"On the contrary, it would fill me with hope."

"I like the sound of that."

William gripped her waist and pulled her closer, while his other hand held hers between them, flush against his chest. She felt the beating of his heart and the quickening of its rhythm.

"*Now* will you tell me when you plan to hold your smuggling evening?" she asked sweetly.

William's face broke out in a smile, his blinding grin only inches from hers. "No."

Pippa frowned. "You do not trust me."

"No, I trust you. I just know that you will not stay away, and I would prefer to keep you safe. Have we not already gone over this?"

She frowned. "Why does Mr. Ainsworth believe he is collecting on a debt?"

"Because he is, in a way."

Pippa tensed, and William did not loosen his hold on her. "He was chasing us on the coast in Dorset when we got into a bit of a battle, us smugglers against his revenue sloop. One of his men was shot and fell into the ocean, and Ainsworth holds us responsible."

Pippa sucked in a quiet breath.

William held her gaze, and she detected pain in his light blue eyes. "We believe that Ainsworth doesn't know who is specifically responsible for that shot, the only reason we have remained safe."

"That is why you've come to Devon."

William nodded. "But it is not why I plan to stay. My father and Roger will not remain much longer, but I intend to. I want to be finished with smuggling; if not for my brother Jack relying on us to unload his next shipment, I would be finished already."

"I did not know you had a brother."

"Oh, yes. He looks exactly like me, though a little shorter and not nearly as handsome."

She smiled up at him. "I take that to mean that your brother is likely very handsome."

His eyes danced. "Do not tell him so. He does not need his chest puffed up further."

"I wonder if the same can be said for you."

"No," he argued, releasing her hand and running his finger

over her jawline. "You can puff my chest up as much as you'd like."

Pippa reveled in the feel of his hand on her and the proximity of their bodies. He was so close, she only needed to lean forward and her lips could touch his. They tingled in anticipation, her heart thudding loudly in her ears. For all of her talk about adventure and excitement, she was nervous about kissing this man.

She needn't have been, though.

William lowered his head and brushed his lips softly over hers. His hand snaked around her neck to tilt her head to the side and kiss her deeper, and Pippa's heart slammed against her breastbone, affection erupting in her. She had never before felt the rush of heat sweep through her body in such a way. She never wanted it to end.

William raised his head and looked at her, his light blue eyes searching hers, serious and gentle.

She leaned up and kissed him one more time, closing her eyes to the world and enjoying the feel of being wholly and utterly his.

Reality beckoned, however, and Pippa broke her hold on him. "I really ought to be getting home. I didn't tell Mabel I was leaving the house, and she's likely to worry soon."

His lips curved into a smile, and they arrested her attention. They'd been so *soft*. "Thank you for coming to warn me."

"Thank *you* for not causing my friend to believe that you were falling in love with two women at the same time."

"Love?"

Pippa's cheeks burned. She hadn't meant to say that, but now she couldn't recant the words. It was too soon for love, but she hoped they would feel that way one day.

She pulled herself free and turned to go. "Until tomorrow, perhaps," she said.

"Pippa?"

"Yes?" she asked, turning back to look at him over her shoulder.

William's gaze had grown serious. "Please stay away from the cove at night. Please."

She didn't respond but instead held his gaze. It was clearly very important to him, and as much as it rankled, she could agree to this for him. She nodded softly and was surprised by the gravity of the relief that fell over his mien.

"Farewell, dear Pippa."

She grinned. "Farewell, William."

CHAPTER 24

illiam wasn't prepared for the bitter cold that swept in seemingly overnight and nipped at his exposed skin like icy hounds. He drew his coat tighter over his neck, grateful for the thick leather gloves that covered his fingers. His hands were stiff but would be immovable without the warmth of the gloves.

Roger pulled the boat down to the surf with the help of Samuel. More men had shown up tonight to help, undoubtedly recruited by Father, and that meant fewer profits for each of them but an easier night. When Burke arrived, Father had been visibly relieved. He was the one man in Collacott who knew everything about the Blakemores' plans but had yet to make his position known. His presence tonight was a comfort and a help.

The weather was cold but dry, and the helping hands plentiful. The sliver of moon sent darkness over the land, but the stars provided enough light to see. It was an ideal final voyage.

William had determined that last week, but had yet to inform anyone aside from Pippa of his intentions. Father seemed to understand that William wanted to be done, but continued to request his help. He wouldn't listen, but Jack might. William planned to inform Jack that if he intended to return to Camden Cove again, it was between him and Father, and William would have no part in it.

He just needed to be firm.

Father could appoint a new leader from the Collacott men if he needed to. Someone would be happy to take the larger cut.

Boots splashed quietly in the water as men filed into the boat, and William joined them. He swung himself onto a seat and took up an oar, ready to row toward the looming dark ship and the swinging lantern in the distance.

He glanced over his shoulder, sweeping the beach once more, but there was no visible sign of Ainsworth. Yet.

But neither was there any sign of Pippa, and that made him grateful.

The remaining men on the beach filed into one of John Caney's smaller boats and followed behind Roger and William. With the extra hands and boat space, they would be finished swiftly. They'd gotten an earlier start, as well, so hopefully they could be done before Ainsworth found them. Whoever had tipped him off likely hadn't given this time for the drop, not when William had changed it just a few days ago. He was only glad that Jack had received the message.

They made their way to Jack's ship and pulled up alongside it. It was always a relief to find his brother unharmed, and the lantern light casting its orange glow over Jack's face was a beacon.

"I'm glad to see you've taken my advice," Jack called, his voice carrying on the wind.

William's men drew his boat close and tied it to the side of the ship. Someone tossed the rope ladder down, and a train of men immediately formed to bring down the merchandise.

It took longer to move the barrels than he would have expected with so many hands, and when they were finally finished, Jack moved to descend the ladder.

THE SMUGGLER OF CAMDEN COVE

"It's not safe," William called. "You ought to leave as soon as you can."

"No, I need to speak with you."

Jack never was one to listen to William's advice. He dropped into William's boat, a wide grin stealing over his face, and they immediately rowed for shore. John Caney's boat pulled up to the ship, and Jack's men started filling it. Men who used to work alongside William, who he called his friends.

Leaving them felt like a betrayal of the worst kind and sat uncomfortably in his stomach. He threw his weight into the oar, rowing hard to reach the beach. The sooner this evening was over with, the better.

Jack climbed over to sit on the bench just in front of him. "I've had word from my man in Bordeaux that he can add tobacco to our shipments."

William swallowed hard. "*Your* shipments."

He couldn't see Jack's face very clearly, but he could well imagine the confusion on his brow. William sucked in a fortifying breath and continued, perfectly aware of the other men—Roger included—listening on the boat. "This is my final run. I'm out after this."

"Has Father—"

"Father has no bearing on my decision." William could hear the biting steel edging his words.

Jack was quiet until they reached the beach. William jumped from the boat and helped Roger pull it up onto the sand. They created another train to empty the boat and pile the barrels into the wagon.

"Jack," Father said jovially, clapping his son on the back. "When will you be back?"

"*Will* I be back?" Jack countered. William felt his stare.

"Of course. What do—"

"Ask Will."

The men were quiet, the tension thick. William shouldn't

have done this so publicly. But perhaps that was an added benefit. Everyone would know.

"I'm finished. This is my final drop."

Father's eyes flashed. "You cannot leave your brother
without help."

"We can discuss this at another time, but I do believe there
are plenty of willing hands. Mine just happen to be done."

John Caney's boat was halfway between Jack's ship and the
shore. They needed to move faster. Something shone on the top
of the cliff, glinting against the starlight, and caught William's
eye. He swore.

"What is it?" Jack asked.

"I think we have a visitor."

Pippa had stayed awake four nights in a row, watching the
shoreline for sign of any ship from her bedroom window. She
knew William didn't want her to be part of it, and she wouldn't
be. She would watch out for him from a distance, and he would
never even know she was there.

She understood that he wanted to protect her. Could he not
understand that she only wished to protect him as well?

That had been the plan at least. When the ship pulled into
the harbor, Pippa had straightened from her slouched position at
her window and donned her scarlet cloak. She let herself outside
and slipped through the trees, avoiding the gravel drive, and
hovered at the edge of the coverage they provided.

Her plan was to watch for Mr. Ainsworth and warn the men
if he appeared. So far, the lanes appeared empty. She shivered in
her cloak, the cold evening air slipping through cracks in her
clothing and chilling her exposed skin.

One of William's boats had made it onto the beach and
finished unloading the barrels, and the second boat was on its

way back from the ship. Urgency tainted the air, buzzing along and making Pippa's body hum. She searched the beach for William's form, but it was too far and too dark to see clearly. A motion caught her eye on the opposite end of the cove near the rock pools, and she peered closer, trying to determine if it was a man or a shadow.

He turned, and light glinted from his eyes. It was most certainly a man, and given his avoidance of the activity on the beach, it was likely Mr. Ainsworth.

Pippa froze. If she ran down to the beach, he would see her coming. If she shouted from above, he would certainly be warned alongside William and the other Collacott men.

The promise she made to William to stay away was irrelevant now that he was in danger.

She needed to sneak down to the sand and warn them quietly. But how? Pippa shed her bright red cloak and immediately regretted not owning one in a darker color. It was freezing outside, and the cold penetrated through her layers of woolen clothing. She hung the cloak on a branch and made her way toward the treacherous path that led from her house directly down to the beach. It was dangerous with the help of sunlight, so she would need to be extremely cautious in the dark.

Voices from the beach reached her when she'd made it halfway down the path, and she wanted to hush the men. Surely Mr. Ainsworth did not yet have enough proof or he would have made himself known. She really wished she'd asked Mac to explain the law surrounding smugglers to her before now. If she understood exactly what it was Mr. Ainsworth needed, she might prevent him from obtaining it.

Pippa's foot slipped on a slick patch of mud, and she grabbed the rock to her side, the rough stone cutting into her palm. Her heart hammered in her chest, and she searched the rock pools for Mr. Ainsworth, but came up empty. Had he already moved on the smugglers? Given their positions waiting on the beach for the second boat, she rather thought that wasn't the case.

Pippa searched the beach, and her gaze snagged on a shadow moving up the main path. Mr. Ainsworth? Was he retreating? Nothing made sense, except that she was immensely grateful she hadn't descended to the beach that same way.

Pippa continued to climb down, taking slower steps despite the urgency skittering through her body. She jumped with both feet when she was only a few feet from the ground and let out a breath of relief. She'd made it.

Hiking up her skirts to her calves, Pippa ran quietly toward the men gathered on the sand.

Someone spotted her, and William whirled around. The starlight was ample this evening and she could see much better than she'd been able to a week ago during the last smuggling evening. Or mission. Whatever it was William called it.

"Pippa?" William asked, his voice incredulous.

She panted, her breaths coming in heaves. "I've come to warn you."

"Ainsworth?" he asked.

She nodded, then realized he might not be able to see her. "Yes. He was over on the rock pools, but he just left."

"Deuce take it," William said.

"It is not good news? He's retreated."

"No, it's not good," William said. "He's likely gone for assistance. We need to get off this beach *now*." He turned toward another man. "Tell Father to get home. Take men with him and hide the barrels."

Father? That man must be his brother.

"What of Caney's load?" another man asked.

"We'll have to dump it. Or return to Jack's ship. We can't very well hide it on the beach."

"Wait," Pippa said. The thread of an idea weaved through her mind. "I think you *can* hide it on the beach."

William did not wait for her to say more. He directed the men to leave and they were off, the wagon rattling along. "Do not take it home," William called softly. He turned for her, and she could see how pained his expression was, how eager he seemed to get her off the beach. "Where?"

Pippa explained about the cave she'd found during her climb a week before. William didn't appear to completely agree that it was ideal.

"It is worth trying," his brother said.

Mr. Caney's boat landed on the surf, and the men formed a line to relieve the boat of the barrels. Pippa led William toward the rock. She began to climb and his hand went around her wrist.

"I know where it is," she argued.

"I will not have your blood on my hands, Pip. I'm climbing. Tell me where to go."

She swallowed her argument. They didn't have time to quarrel. She directed him to the right location and pointed out where the narrow cave was.

"This just might work." William sounded pleased, and the men made quick work of heaving the barrels up the beach. When William landed on the sand again, he took her hand and squeezed her leather-clad fingers.

"You broke your promise."

"Aren't you glad I did?"

He chuckled, the warm sound having lost the edge of concern he held earlier. "I will not dignify that comment with a response."

"Are you planning to introduce me?" a man asked, stepping up to William's side. The sliver of moon provided enough light to make out his sharp jaw and dark hair.

"Jack, this is my friend, Miss Sheffield."

"Friend?" Jack asked.

Pippa and William were both silent, and Jack laughed. "Ah, I see. Well, I look forward to the day we can meet in the sunlight, Miss Sheffield. You sound absolutely lovely."

She grinned. From what she could make out, Jack did look very much like his brother. Handsome and dashing, though not quite as handsome as William.

"It will be my pleasure," she said, dipping a soft curtsy.

William clapped Jack on the back. "We need to get you to your ship."

Light appeared at the top of the cliff and Pippa's body stilled. A handful of men walked the cliff path toward the cove, torches held high above their heads.

"Ainsworth is back."

CHAPTER 25

*W*illiam got Jack into the boat with John Caney and a few others and pushed them into the waves. He remained on the beach with Roger and Pippa, prepared to meet the law men. Three torches came toward them, bobbing down the path and onto the beach, and William crossed his arms over his chest. He wished Pippa wasn't at his side, but she had no way to escape. These men were going to search every bit of this beach.

"Good evening, gentlemen," William said jovially. "What can we do for you?"

"Do not play games with me," Ainsworth spat. His eyes were crazed, a smile playing over his lips. "You've been caught."

William lifted his arms in a gesture to indicate that he had nothing to hide. "Forgive me, is this your beach? I did not realize we were trespassing."

An older man with a white mustache stepped forward. "What are you doing here?"

"I came to greet my brother, but he needed to be on his way." William indicated the ship waiting in the harbor. "I'm sorry you missed him."

"And his goods? Where are those?" Ainsworth asked.

"I'm not sure what you mean."

The man with the white mustache nodded to Pippa. "Good evening, Miss Sheffield. Does your brother-in-law know you are here?"

She didn't respond to his question. "Good evening, Mr. James."

Mr. James held her gaze before his hand came up, waving his men forward. "Search everywhere." He looked to William. "You won't mind waiting here while we search the beach, will you?"

"Of course not. We have nothing to hide."

That wasn't strictly true.

Ainsworth remained near them while the others searched the beach. They started with the empty boat and combed the rocky edges. When they reached the rock pools, William could sense Pippa's apprehension. He reached for her hand and slid his around it, holding her and squeezing her fingers in support. She curled her hand around his, and he could feel the tension leave her in waves.

Pippa shivered, her shoulders shaking, and William slipped his coat from his arms and laid it over her.

"I cannot take this."

"Yes, you can." He was glad when she didn't argue further. The presence of the law must have subdued her. It certainly had that effect on him.

They stood on the cold, quiet beach for another half-hour, waiting while the men searched. William's gut tightened when the torches neared the cliff-cave, and Pippa's fingers clutched his firmly until the men passed the hiding place.

Caney's boat splashed in the surf, and he pulled it up onto the sand with Samuel's help before joining them. Caney must have done some smuggling in his earlier years, for he'd known exactly what needed doing and how to appear unaffected by Ainsworth's presence.

The white-mustached man trudged back toward them, a frustrated look on his face that he directed to Ainsworth. "Nothing."

"No, that cannot be. I saw it with my own eyes."

Mr. James shook his head. "Nothing." He turned to Pippa. "I will see you home, Miss Sheffield. Mac would have my neck if I left you here."

She seemed to weigh his words and agree. She released William's hand, and he wanted to reach for her again, but instead watched her leave at Mr. James's side, his torch lighting the way up the rocky path.

Ainsworth stepped forward and grabbed William by the cravat so swiftly, he hadn't seen it coming. "Where did you stash it?"

Roger's arm reared back, and he punched Ainsworth in the jaw, forcing the man to let go of William before he fell on the sand. Roger shook out his fist.

"Thank you."

"Don't thank me yet."

Ainsworth rose again on unsteady feet. "One of you killed my friend, and I *refuse* to allow you to get away with it."

"You were shooting at us as well," William said calmly.

Ainsworth rubbed his jaw. "But none of you died."

What did he expect? That Roger would step forward and admit to his wrongdoing? "We're deeply sorry for your loss, but that is where our cooperation ends."

Ainsworth glared. "I don't care how long it takes. I will peg you for this. I will peg you for *something*."

"Good luck," Roger said.

William grabbed his forearm, hoping the action was warning enough. It wasn't wise to press a revenue man. Although . . . if Ainsworth was still a revenue man, why was he here alone, depending on help from the local constable?

"Won't your captain be needing you?" William asked.

Ainsworth stilled. "No."

"Why not?"

"He doesn't need me to return right away. He's given me leave as long as I need it. So do not fear, I have time on my side."

His commanding officer had given him leave and all the time he needed. That was not usual, and the pieces suddenly all clicked together. "You are not here on an official capacity, are you?"

Ainsworth did not respond immediately, which was all the response William needed. "Why is that?" he pressed. "Did your commanding officer not sanction this trip?"

"It did not need sanctioning."

"Because it isn't official," Roger said, understanding what William had figured out. "You are not here on an official, legal capacity. You are merely settling the debt. Yet you do not even know who is guilty."

"You are," Ainsworth spat. "Both of you. Your whole crew is responsible. If you would only follow the law, Nathan would still be alive."

That hit William like a punch in the gut. How many times had he thought the very same thing? If his family had followed the law, his mother would still be alive.

"I understand your frustration—"

Anger rolled from Ainsworth in seething waves. "You could *never* understand."

"I do, actually. I lost my mother in a similar manner. She came out with us and her life was taken, shot by a revenue officer in the middle of unloading—" William cleared his throat. "When we were overtaken on the beach. She shouldn't even have been there. I *do* understand."

Fire poured from Ainsworth's eyes.

William's heart reached out to the man, to the pain and loss he'd experienced. "I cannot take back the actions of the night or restore your friend to you, but I can extend my deepest, heartfelt apologies."

"You and your apologies can *hang*."

William shook his head. There was no reaching Ainsworth through his grief. William was sorry for what had occurred, and he understood the pain and frustration Ainsworth likely felt now, but he could do no more than apologize, and he had.

"Come," he said. "Let's go home."

"No." Ainsworth's voice was dangerous and low. His chest heaved in deep, shallow breaths, his eyes growing wild in the low light. "I won't let you get away with this. If I must enact justice myself, then so be it." He extended his arm and light from another torch behind them shone on the steel in his shaky hand.

He had a gun.

The shot rang out before William could dive for safety, the explosion of light and sound accompanying it and ringing from the cove. Pain sliced through William's side, and he stumbled, falling to the sand with a hard thud.

Roger leapt forward and tackled Ainsworth to the ground. They wrestled, their blurry bodies sideways from William's view lying on the sand. He wanted to get up, but his limbs would not respond to his wishes. He watched Roger tug the gun from Ainsworth's grip and hit him over the head with the heavy steel. Footsteps ran toward them, heavy and muted by the sand, and William looked up toward the cliffside. He hoped Pippa made it inside before the shot rang out, that she was safe in her house.

William struggled to remain alert. People swam before him, colors blending into darkness despite the fire torches lighting the scene until everything went black.

CHAPTER 26

*P*ippa stopped in the entryway of her home, her body freezing in place. "That was a gunshot."

Mr. James cocked his head to the side. "I'm not sure . . ."

She speared him with a look. "It was, and you know it." Pippa brushed past him, back out into the cold. "We must go back."

Mr. James took her by the arm, his strong grip holding her by his side. "I will return to the cove, but you stay here, Miss Sheffield."

"No, if it was William . . ." She would not allow herself to complete that thought. "I need to go back."

Footsteps sounded on the stairs behind them, and Pippa's eyes drifted shut. Now there was *no* possibility she would be allowed out of the house. She would have to climb out her window or some other nonsense. She tugged her arm free and Mr. James released her, albeit begrudgingly.

"James?" Mac called, confused. He approached in his dressing gown and stockings, his eyes alert despite the late hour. "Pip? What is going on?"

"There was a bit of a scuffle down at the cove," Mr. James said, watching her warily. "Smugglers."

Mac approached, a stern look on his brow. "Who?"

"Blakemores, Caneys, Burkes. A whole lot of them, and those were only the ones I saw."

Mac's mouth flattened into a grim line. "You caught them?"

There was a slight hesitation before the constable said, "We found nothing. They were free to go."

Was that relief that flattened Mac's shoulders? Pippa squared her own. "We heard a gunshot, though, just a minute ago. I need to go back. I need to be certain—"

"You are not leaving this house. Especially not if there were shots fired."

"But Mac—"

"*No.*" He ran a hand over his face. "You stay here, Pip. I'll go." He turned back for the stairs.

"I'll go with you," Mr. James said, exhaustion lining his words.

"Give me a few minutes, James. I'll be right down."

Pippa watched her brother-in-law retreat and looked back to Mr. James. He was an older man, undoubtedly frustrated to have been woken up in the night to deal with smugglers who appeared innocent. He watched her shrewdly, as if he could read her thoughts and knew she was determining whether or not she could slip past him and run toward the beach before he could catch her.

"Your coat is wet," he said, indicating the heavy, black coat on her shoulders. She looked down. She'd forgotten that William had given it to her.

"Oh, it isn't mine. My cloak is just outside hanging on those trees, and I ought to retrieve it."

Mr. James smiled. "No, ma'am. I can see precisely what you are trying to do, and I will have none of it."

"I am in earnest. My cloak is hanging on a tree just there."

She pointed toward the trees that lined the drive and waited for Mr. James to follow her line of vision. Once his attention was firmly on the trees, Pippa slid William's coat smoothly from her shoulders, hiked her skirts up to her shins, and ran.

Mr. James whirled, reaching for her, and she felt his fingers brush her gown, but he did not find any purchase. The nearness of him lit a fire beneath her feet, and Pippa ran harder, the dark pressing in on her as she left the warmth of Mr. James's torch and followed the familiar path toward Camden Cove.

Mac would be along soon, and he would certainly be angry with her, but she could not simply sit at home and wait for news. Pippa picked her way speedily down the path which her feet knew well, despite the darkness. The men were grouped exactly where she'd left them, huddled around a man on the sand while another was being held a few feet off.

But where was William?

The torch moved, lighting Mr. Ainsworth's angry face as Roger held his arms tightly behind his back, pressing the side of his face into the sand.

If Mr. Ainsworth shot the gun and Roger was holding him back, *where* was William? Hot fear pulsed in Pippa's belly, and she shoved the men aside, snaking her way between them in order to see who had fallen.

William.

He lay unconscious on the sand, red staining his chest and falling over the sandy pebbles.

Pippa screamed, falling to her knees. She pressed a hand to his heart, closing her eyes and listening for the beating. It was there—weak, but it was there.

"Pippa," Mac yelled, coming to stop behind her, panting. He seemed to take in the entire scene. Roger, the law man, William, shot and on the ground. "Has a doctor been sent for?"

No positive answer met him, and Mac swore. "John, ride for Dr. Garvey. With haste!"

"At once. Of course." Mr. Caney jumped up and ran toward the path.

Mac turned and shouted. "Take a horse from my stables if you need to, and direct Garvey to my house."

Mr. Caney lifted a hand in acknowledgment and took off, Samuel just behind him.

Mac had taken control of the situation swiftly, and Pippa was grateful, for she'd seemed to have forgotten how to breathe. She took William's soft, cool hand in hers and squeezed his fingers.

Mac crouched beside her, speaking gently. "We need to move him, Pip."

"I know," she said, the words scratchy and hard-edged leaving her tired throat.

Mac took William under the shoulders and Roger stepped over to take him by the legs. Pippa looked up swiftly. "If you're here—"

"They've got him," Roger said solemnly. He looked over his shoulder and Pippa followed his gaze. Mr. James had secured Mr. Ainsworth's hands behind his back and was leading him away, likely to the holding cell in Collacott until he could be taken to the magistrate tomorrow.

The men heaved William up and carried him slowly toward Camden Court, Pippa following close behind. When they reached the top of the rise, Mac turned his head just enough to steal her attention away from William's ghostly pallor.

"Run ahead and prepare a room," Mac asked, his breathing labored.

"Which one?"

"Any."

Pippa nodded. She lifted her hem and ran toward the house. Surely Mabel wouldn't care where they laid the invalid, but he would need access to hot water and towels and a warm fire. She let herself inside and ran upstairs as quickly as she could until she located the room of their kitchen maid, Alice.

"Alice, I need you."

"Yes?" she asked, rushing to sit up.

"William Blakemore has been shot. We'll need boiling water and fresh linens. I'm going to prepare the prince's suite now."

"Yes, ma'am. Right away," Alice said sleepily. She was out of her bed before Pippa had turned away.

She didn't know how yet, but she was going to save William. He was not dying tonight.

CHAPTER 27

*P*ain. All William could decipher was the pain radiating from his chest and moving down his side. He slipped in and out of groggy, broken sleep, again and again to the fiery torment that welcomed him. There was softness, too, in the gentleness of Pippa's voice and the cool towel on his forehead. But the pain was insurmountable, and he wished it would end.

Soft singing slipped through his discomfort, soothing his mind and body. William latched onto it like it carried the freedom from his burdens and allowed the sweet melody to carry him from his pain.

Darkness crept in, and he was gone again.

Pippa sat on the chair at the head of William's bed and dipped a cloth into the cool water before laying it on his forehead again. His skin was hot to the touch, sweat beading and mixing with the cool water and rolling down his temples. "If you would wake up, William, then I could get more soup into your stomach."

He didn't oblige her.

Pippa watched him struggle through a fever all day and well into the following night. She bathed his forehead and sang softly to him whenever they were left alone. She didn't have the most pleasant voice, but when she sang quietly enough, it could be deemed soothing. Or so she hoped.

"Pip?"

Her soft hymn came to a halting stop. Mabel stood in the doorway, Mac a giant shadow behind her. "Yes?"

"Will you come with us?" Mabel asked. "We need to talk."

Those four words—*we need to talk*—never boded well. Either Pippa was in trouble or Mabel intended to ask a favor of her. "Of course."

She dragged the cloth over William's warm forehead one last time, her gaze raking over his solemn, rested features. He was just as handsome in his sleep, his dark lashes fanning over tanned cheeks. She really would like to kiss those cheeks. If only he wasn't unconscious.

Pippa left William behind, her heart sitting squarely in his motionless hands. Mabel stood in the corridor, her mouth pinched in concern. She led the way toward her own bedchamber and closed the door after they'd each filed inside. "This is the only place we can be assured of privacy, though I cannot guarantee that my children will not barge through that door with little hesitation."

"You mean without any hesitation at all, I believe," Mac corrected, crossing toward the chairs before the fireplace and indicating for the women to be seated.

This felt formal, uncomfortable. "Are you vexed with me?" Pippa asked. "I feel as though I must prepare for a scolding."

Mabel shook her head. "You're far too old for a scolding. Though I do think you ought to avoid Mr. Blakemore's bedroom unless you are chaperoned."

"What sort of rumors would arise from me dabbing his forehead with a wet cloth?"

"I am less concerned with the nursing, Pip, and far more worried about the relationship between you and Mr. Blakemore." Mabel sucked in a breath and released it slowly. "What exactly is that man to you?"

Relationship. The word was pregnant with meaning but impossible for Pippa to define. He'd kissed her—or had *she* kissed *him*?—but that bit of information would only worry Mabel further. Pippa knew she wanted William in her life, that the terror that swept through her when she found him injured was not akin to anything she'd ever felt before.

"I care for him," she finally said. "I believe he cares for me as well."

"Do you not think it is too soon to know that?"

"No." Pippa gripped her hands together on her lap. Mabel loved her and only wanted what was best for her, but she'd somehow forgotten how it felt to fall in love. "I know my own mind."

"That is indisputable," Mac muttered. He narrowed his gaze. "The man was most assuredly breaking the law. Does that not worry you?"

"He doesn't wish to, not anymore. But he couldn't leave his brother without assistance. He has been forced to balance his family loyalty with his own private reservations, and I do not envy him that."

"Nor do I," Mac agreed. "Have you considered your father's stance on the matter?"

"According to Gram, Father has enjoyed his share of smuggled wine, so I am not entirely sure he would have strong opinions in this case."

Mac grinned, looking to Mabel, and she nodded confirmation. "It is a difficult thing to judge when our parents grew up enjoying the fruits of smuggling themselves. They wouldn't have been able to afford tea or sugar otherwise."

"Or wine," Pippa added.

"Regardless," Mabel said, "you cannot be alone with the man, not until you are husband and wife."

Those words strung together brought an image to Pippa's mind of William and her in the little Blakemore cottage, Pippa tending the garden while William brushed down their horses after a ride on the beach. Such a picture of domesticity had never called to her before as it now did when William made up the other half of the equation.

"Does our union have your blessing, Mac?" she asked.

He looked at Pippa hard. "I like the man, but for something this important, I think you'll need to write to your father."

Pippa had already written a letter, but she was waiting for William to wake before she sent it.

"But you will write one, too?" she pressed. If Mac approved, she knew her father would also.

Mac's mouth ticked up in a smile. "I will write one, too."

She breathed out her relief. After William's illegal behavior, Pippa had worried about whether or not her family would approve, about whether or not they would make this difficult. Mac didn't appear entirely at ease with the situation, but he must have respected William's character enough to look past it, to do his best to be understanding and give the man a chance to prove himself. William had promised to leave smuggling behind. Now he needed to heal and then prove himself a man of his word.

"Are you certain Mr. Blakemore holds you in a similar regard?" Mabel asked.

"Yes."

"Then surely a little more caution regarding his bedchamber will not ruin your relationship with the man."

A knock sounded at the door, and Mac stood to answer it.

226

Mabel leaned closer and lowered her voice. She likely wanted to slip her last piece of advice in before the children commanded her attention. "Father has entrusted us to protect you, and your reputation is part of that, Pip."

"I understand."

"Then will you please be more mindful in the future?"

Mac spoke, saving her from needing to reply. "Mr. Blakemore is here again, and he is not pleased."

Oh, drat. Not this again.

Mabel stood. "Shall I come with you to speak to him?"

Mac's mouth pressed into a firm line. "Perhaps you can make sense of the situation better. He clearly did not appreciate my explanation."

Mabel followed her husband out of the room and down the stairs, and Pippa joined them. William's father had come by late last night, angry that William had not been taken to Ravenwood Cottage directly.

Mr. Blakemore stood in the entryway, leaning heavily on his cane, a scowl dragging his face down. "Has he awoken?"

"I am a man of my word, sir," Mac said, his voice solid and steady. "I will send someone for you the moment your son wakes."

"No, Mr. Blakemore," Mabel soothed. "He is still very much asleep."

Mr. Blakemore's eyes shifted from Mabel to Mac. "If he is sleeping, I do not see the harm in taking him home with me. He should be with his family."

"I do not understand either," Mac said. "But Dr. Garvey recommended leaving William in that bed until he is better, and I think we ought to trust the word of the physician."

That was a difficult point to argue with. Pippa could see the distress in Mr. Blakemore's eyes, and she pitied his concern. "Would you like to come up and sit beside his bed for a while?"

The man looked at her sharply. The room was tense until Mr.

Blakemore nodded, and Pippa turned to lead him upstairs. Mabel and Mac followed, and they all went up to the sick room but remained in the corridor, the door open, while Mr. Blakemore went inside.

Mr. Blakemore lowered himself onto the chair beside William's bed.

Mac cleared his throat. "We will leave you now. You are welcome to stay as long as you wish."

"I will stay with him," Pippa said quietly. Her heart reached out to the man. She understood how difficult it was to see William hurt and unconscious and to wish he would only just open his eyes. They had fluttered a few times, as though he were almost awake, but each time, he'd slipped back into a deep sleep again.

Mabel looked as though she meant to argue, but Mac put his hand around her shoulders and steered her away.

Fire cracked and popped in the hearth, the orange glow casting over Mr. Blakemore's worried countenance. He rested both hands over the lion-shaped cane head and frowned.

"We can have a room made up for you if you'd like to remain here with your son," Pippa said.

Mr. Blakemore's gaze shifted to her and away again. "I will return home, but I trust he is in good hands." It was spoken like a threat, and Pippa brushed off his abrasive tone. He was a concerned parent.

"Oh yes. I've hardly left his side."

Mr. Blakemore's attention rested on his son again, not betraying the least surprise at this admission. They sat in silence, the time stretching, unbroken except for the popping of the fire and the steady breathing of the invalid.

"Dr. Garvey mentioned that he believed William will make a full recovery, Mr. Blakemore. I assure you that we are doing everything we can to aid in his comfort and healing."

"I believe you."

"We've yet to see Roger—"

"Roger has left."

Pippa stilled. "Where has he gone?"

"Away. He went to join Jack on the boat." Mr. Blakemore glanced up sharply. He likely hadn't meant to reveal so much, but all Pippa could think about was Lily.

"Does he intend to return?"

"No."

She sucked in a quiet breath. Did Lily know of this? Was her heart broken?

If it wasn't so late at night, Pippa would go to her.

Mr. Blakemore stood. "I should be on my way."

Pippa laid a hand on his forearm. "I promise that we will send someone to inform you the moment William stirs."

"Thank you."

He left, and Pippa hovered in the doorway, hesitant to leave William's room. Despite her promise to Mabel, she didn't want to be away from him. If someone was to bathe his forehead in cool water, why could it not be her? Was it really so much better if a servant saw to the task?

Footsteps on the stairs recalled her attention.

"Please wake soon," she whispered quietly, then turned to follow Mr. Blakemore downstairs, leaving William's sickroom behind.

CHAPTER 28

When William blinked his eyes open again, soft light fell through the window and the fiery pain in his side had been banked to low, smoldering embers. He looked about the unfamiliar room until his gaze snagged on Pippa, slouched in a chair just near the head of his bed, her head tilted at a seemingly uncomfortable angle as she slept.

He didn't wish to wake her, no matter his numerous questions.

Instead, William set to discovering what had changed in his body. He lifted the sheets to find a bandaged chest, but despite the intense pain in his side, all seemed intact.

"You're awake." Pippa's soft voice reached into his chest and wrapped around his heart, warming him from inside.

He turned his head and met her steady gaze. "Indeed." His voice was hoarse and rough.

She let out a shuddering breath. Dropping her feet to the floor, she leaned forward and took his hand in both of hers. "I was so worried."

"I'm a fighter," William said, smiling. "It would take more than a gunshot to the chest to knock me out."

Pippa shook her head. "You are mad. And the gunshot missed your chest, thank heavens. It was lower and much safer. What can I get for you? Water? Are you hungry?"

His stomach rolled at the thought of food, and Pippa must have read his corresponding expression.

She tilted her head softly to the side. "Perhaps only a little broth? And some bread?"

William squeezed her fingers gently. "I don't wish for you to leave."

"I should probably leave before Mabel wakes, or she'll be vexed with me again."

"And why is she vexed?"

"Because she told me to stay out of your room unless I'm chaperoned. It's not my fault you are in the room next to mine, William. Well," she paused scrunching her nose, "actually, I suppose it is. I chose your chamber when Mac carried you home."

"Mac carried me?" William could not wrap his mind around the image that conjured.

"With Roger's help."

"Ah, Roger. Of course." He cleared his throat and Pippa jumped up to hand him a glass of water. She slid her hand behind his neck and helped him to lean forward while tipping the cool, refreshing water down his parched throat. Once she finished, she set the water back on the little table beside her and lowered herself in her chair.

"You've been asleep for two days, William. We were all worried you weren't going to wake up."

"I've been awake a few times."

"But never like this," she argued.

"No, not like this." All he remembered from those wakeful moments was the burning fire and pain and exhaustion, and Pippa's sweet voice. "But you were there."

She looked surprised. "You were alert enough to know?"

"I know you sang to me."

Pippa's cheeks flushed scarlet. "Please tell me you cannot remember that. William, I do not sing well."

"I thought you sang beautifully."

Pippa laughed. "You most certainly were in a dream."

"It was a very enjoyable dream." He thought of the fire in his chest. "For the most part."

She rose. "I'll go fetch you something to eat."

"Pippa."

"Yes?"

"Where is my father?"

She stilled. "He is at home. At Ravenwood. I promised him we would send word the moment you awoke."

Pippa moved to rise, and William lifted his hand to stall her. "No, not yet."

"He was so concerned and actually a little angry that you'd been brought here instead of your own cottage, but Mac smoothed things over. Roger is gone, though."

"Did he say where to?"

"He went to join Jack." She pulled a frustrated expression. "I can only imagine how heartbroken Lily is."

William made a noncommittal sound. Sending Roger off with Jack was a wise move until things died down here. At least they could be sure that Ainsworth would no longer be on their tail.

"Yes, of course that would come as no surprise to you." She cleared her throat and seemed to decide between staying and leaving the room. Sucking a breath into her lungs, she faced him with determination. "I need to know what you intend to do. I've . . . I've fought for you, and for us, and I need to know now if it was in vain."

"What do you mean?" William struggled to rise, and she crossed to him quickly and pressed against his good shoulder.

"No, do not try to sit up. Dr. Garvey warned us to help you move very slowly after you awoke."

He cared little for the doctor's directions when faced with her pronouncement. "What do you mean, Pip? Who did you fight?"

She lowered herself on the edge of his mattress, a gentle line forming between her eyebrows. "Mabel and Mac are a little concerned about our . . . relationship. That was their term for it. I fought for us, but I need to know now if it was in vain."

William found her hand and squeezed gently. Her gentle blush was endearing, and he longed to pull her into his arms and kiss away her concern. "I love you, Pippa."

A smile swept over her lips. "Oh, good. I was so worried after Roger left that you'd go as well. I didn't dare hope that you meant what you'd said, that you truly wished to build a life here. For I could never leave Collacott."

"Could you move into a tiny, damp cottage near the sea?"

Pippa beamed, closing her other hand over the top of his. "Yes."

"Then tell me who I am to ask for permission for your hand, and I will ask this moment. Shall I write a letter to your father or call Mac in here?"

"We better wait until Mac's awoken, and I've already asked for you."

"Of course you have."

She leaned close. "They're wary, but they trust me. Mac will grant permission in my father's stead so long as you promise not to take me far away from them."

"I can promise that. For now." His dry lips widened into a smile, and Pippa reached over to move his hair away from his eyes.

She regarded him thoughtfully, her dark navy eyes sparkling with warmth that he wanted to lose himself in. "I am so very glad you've awoken."

"As am I."

William slid his hand around the back of her head and gently pulled her down until her lips met his. The softest brush at first, and then with more pressure, speaking to how deeply he'd missed her. Heat shot through his chest and hammered at his heart, and he tugged her closer, unable to reach his fill.

Pippa's hands framed his face, and her gentle fingers were lost in his hair. She pulled back and rested her forehead against his. "I don't wish for you to be hurt so soon after waking."

"I think you are more medicine than damage, Pippa."

"Well, in that case." She leaned down and kissed him again, filling his body with warmth and light. When she pulled away, she was breathless, and he had never felt so complete.

"I think I just might love you, William."

"That is good, for as I've previously mentioned, I most assuredly love you."

The door in the next room opened and a silent pause preceded a feminine shout. "Pippa!"

She squealed, jumping up from the side of William's bed and smoothing her skirts. She ran a hand over her hair and tucked loose pieces back into the knot at the nape of her neck. The door creaked open, and Mrs. Mackenzie poked her head in. "Pip, there you are—oh! William is awake."

He hadn't realized that her family had taken to calling him by his Christian name, but he liked the familiarity very much.

"He is, and I was just about to go downstairs and send someone to inform his father before I fetch him something to eat."

"Thank you, Pippa. I'll go with you. Is there anything else you need, William? I will send for Dr. Garvey, too, so he can look at you again."

"Thank you, Mrs. Mackenzie."

"Oh, please do call me Mabel. Apparently, we are soon to be brother and sister if Pip is to be believed."

William grinned. "I would like that very much."

He could not tell if it was real or imagined, but he thought he saw relief pass over her face.

Pippa shot him a triumphant smile before following her sister from the room, and William was content. He had fallen in love, and it was returned. He was finished with smuggling, and his father had seemed to accept that—surely that was why Roger had been sent away. And he was going to marry Pippa, and they were going to be happy in their little cottage by the sea.

EPILOGUE

$\mathcal{P}$ippa leaned forward and corrected the pink blossom in Elinor's hair before it could fall onto the ground. She'd taken it from her own hair earlier that day and tucked it into Elinor's plait, and her niece had absolutely beamed. "There you are," Pippa said, wrapping her hands over Elinor's shoulders. "Now you won't lose your flower."

Elinor turned and wrapped her tiny arms around Pippa's waist. "I'm going to miss you so dearly."

"I will live but a ten-minute walk away, and you will see me far more often than you'd like."

"And *now* I have a new uncle, too," Elinor said, an echo of the conversation they'd had many times before during the previous few months.

"An uncle who likes to *eat little children for breakfast,*" William said, picking Elinor up and tickling her while she squealed.

"Save me!"

Pippa took her niece from her husband's arms and set her back on the ground. William made as if he were going to chase the little girl, and she ran off, squealing. The sun was setting over the ocean just beyond where their celebration was taking place, just outside of Camden Court. Pink and orange streaked the sky, making the earth glow warm and hazy.

William hooked his hand around Pippa's waist. "I've been looking for you everywhere."

"I was busy." She rested her head against his shoulder and looked up into his pale blue eyes. "I spoke to Mrs. Burke for a while, and she agreed to allow Dr. Mason to look at Tommy while he was here. He did an evaluation and found nothing wrong with the boy. He believes Tommy ought to be careful to avoid those who are ill because he has a tendency to become sick himself, but it is nothing detrimental."

"That must be an inordinate relief."

She nodded, her forehead resting on his neck. "It is. I'm glad she agreed. I told her it was our wedding gift, and she threatened to take the handkerchiefs she embroidered for us back."

"Did she take them?"

"No. They possess our initials." Pippa grinned.

William gazed down into her eyes, seeing through her as he always had done. "Do you wish we would have waited until your father could have joined us?"

"Another eight months? No." Her heart squeezed. "I miss him, and I do wish he could have been here today. But he was clear in his letter that he was happy to meet you later, and I do believe whatever Mac wrote to my father went a great distance in gathering his approval."

"Remind me to thank Mac later."

Pippa chuckled. "Now we must plan for a Season in London so we can take Lily and find someone to help her forget Roger."

"I do believe I owe her that much after bringing the man to Collacott," William said ruefully. "Though perhaps we can hire your sister's friends to find Lily a man. They are very . . . thorough."

Pippa frowned. "What do you mean by that?"

"They examined me rigidly while you were with the Burkes, but I do believe I've passed muster."

"Oh, thank goodness. How awkward it would have been to have to leave you *after* the wedding."

His voice rumbled low, and she felt it through his chest. "You would never."

"Well, if Giulia, Hattie, and Amelia did not like you, I'm afraid—"

William swung her up into his arms, robbing her of words. He silenced her further with a hearty kiss that turned slow and smooth. Pippa wrapped her arms around his neck and leaned into him, her feet dangling in the air. When he leaned back, his lips held a rakish grin. "It is a good thing they love me then, eh?"

"It's a good thing *I* love you, sir."

"That, too."

"Will you put me down, now?"

"No." William turned back toward the party, holding Pippa in his arms. He cleared his throat until he had garnered most of the attention from the patrons of their wedding party, and said, "Thank you all, and good night."

The group cheered for the newly married couple as William weaved his way through the crowd and onto the lane that would lead toward Ravenwood Cottage.

"I love you, Mrs. Blakemore."

Pippa's heart soared. "And I love you."

AUTHOR'S NOTE

During the 18th century the English coast saw a spike in smuggling that correlated with the exorbitant taxes on sugar, tea, and alcohol. According to contemporary estimates, ⅘ of all tea drunk in England in the 18th century was imported illegally, which is understandable when one considers that tea grew to be taxed nearly 70% of its original price by the mid 1700's. Tax laws changed before the start of the Regency era that cut smuggling down significantly, but characters like Pippa's father and Gram would have grown up before that time. They would have been familiar with smuggled goods and accepted them readily.

The relationship citizens had with the law was different back then, as the law keepers were structured in such a different way than we have today. Entire coastal towns would come together in support of smuggling, careful to physically turn away from illegal activity or even blindfold themselves when participating in moving barrels so they could later claim ignorance ("I saw nothing!"). Many people could not afford goods without smuggling, and that went a long way in creating communities that widely accepted it. The hiding place in the back of the Collacott church is a nod to the real vicars in history who drank smuggled wine—good men of God who lived in a world where smuggling was not the black and white issue we see it as today.

Smuggled goods were widely accepted and the practice was strong until the 1840's. Though smugglers themselves some-times carried dark reputations and cause for fear. Black Heart Blakemore mildly represents some of those smugglers, but his injury and age made him no longer a threat.

My research took me to places that told stories of smugglers who were caught and turned on their own men in order to escape the noose, thus becoming revenue men themselves. The revenue men were an assortment who ranged from good, law-abiding men to those who were merely there to save their own skin. It wasn't uncommon for them to have a bad reputation. Many townspeople would take turns distracting revenue men in order for their neighbors to hide smuggled goods.

I found the 19th century's moral relationship with smug-gling fascinating and hoped to portray the gray area it presented to the people of the day. The many facets and opinions were represented throughout this story in William's change in posi-tion, in Pippa and the Mackenzies' desire to understand and form an opinion on the matter, and in the way the Caneys participated and the constable was relieved not to have been forced to arrest anyone. I hope it taught you a little something about the peoples' relationship with smuggling and gave you something to think about.

Source: *Smuggling in the British Isles: A History,* Richard Platt

ACKNOWLEDGMENTS

None of my books would ever make it to publication without the support and love I feel from my Heavenly Father. When I was in the depths of drafting this story, I had to lean on Him especially hard, and I know with a surety that God cares about the little things I care about, like my writing and my books, because He loves me.

My husband is a close second in regards to support, and he most certainly cares about the little things I care about as well. I would not have been able to produce this book without his understanding and grace.

Thank you to Jacque and Jenny, your insights and edits are always enormously helpful. Jenny, I owe the polish to you! You are the grammar queen.

Deborah, thanks for reading this book even though you didn't have time. Although no one is surprised by this, since it's a book inspired by Poldark. Your insight is incredibly valuable, and I appreciate you holding my hand up until the end with those last minute edits!

Thank you to my beta readers, Melanie Atkinson, Whitney Hurst, Heidi Stott, Brooke Hampton, and Rachel Stones. You were all so helpful, as always, and I appreciate your thoughts.

Finally, thank you to the ARC readers, the bookstagrammers, and all of you readers who enjoyed this story and left a kind review.

There wasn't supposed to be a fifth Ladies of Devon story. Readers, I wrote this one for you.

ABOUT THE AUTHOR

Kasey Stockton is a staunch lover of all things romantic. She doesn't discriminate between genres and enjoys a wide variety of happily ever afters. Drawn to the Regency period at a young age when gifted a copy of *Sense and Sensibility* by her grandmother, Kasey initially began writing Regency romances. She has since written in a variety of genres, but all of her titles fall under clean romance. A native of northern California, she now resides in Texas with her own prince charming and their three children. When not reading, writing, or binge-watching chick flicks, she enjoys running, cutting hair, and anything chocolate.

Made in United States
North Haven, CT
25 April 2024

51740374R00157